AN IRANIAN ODYSSEY

ASEMANA
BOOKS

AN IRANIAN ODYSSEY

Rana Soleimani

Translated from the Persian
by Feridon Rashidi

ASEMANA
BOOKS

Toronto, Canada

FIRST EDITION

Published by ASEMANA BOOKS

ISBN: 978-1-0690210-3-8

Book Design: Asemana Books

Cover Art: Asemana Books

To find out more about our authors and books visit: www.asemanabooks.ca

ASEMANA
BOOKS

Contents

1

I am lying on my back on the wood planks at the end of the boardwalk that stretches to the middle of the pond.

The sunlight glistens on my bare skin spread with suncream. I listen to the trilling of the thrushes that sing among the foliage. I watch the white clouds scattered lazily high in the sky that slowly change their form – now a horse, then an umbrella that changes into some other formless shapes. After the morning swim and the warmth, I feel drowsy. I shade my eyes with my arm and put my headphones on and listen to a song by Bob Dylan:

> *How many roads must a man walk down*
> *Before you call him a man?*
> *How many seas must a white dove sail*
> *Before she sleeps in the sand?*

I think I slept for a few minutes and did not hear a sound. It was as if I was floating in a pleasant void. I sense a shadow falling on my face. I open my eyes. It is my son standing beside me. I take the headphones from my ears.

'I've been calling you a thousand times, Mum,' he pants. 'I'm hungry!' My hands and feet have gone numb. I raise my hand to him to help me stand up. Being merely nine years old, he has a strong and athletic body. His eyes are shining from under his umbrella-like brown hair. They look like prisms that, instead of absorbing light, reflect it. He pulls me up. When I stand up, I stretch my body. My hair has become oily with the sun-cream I've rubbed my body with. I tie it up tightly with a hairband.

I follow my son. With Swedish-sounding words coming from his larynx, he rattles on non-stop! It has been a while since he has been mixing the 'sh' and 'kh' speech sounds in a melodious way. This is something I will never be able to do. I am sure that language ability is innate rather than acquired, inborn as mathematical and musical aptitudes are.

We pass the tame seagulls and ducks lounging along the pond under the hot sun. The birds ignore us as we walk on the creaking boardwalk. We come to a large area in the park covered with grass. I smell the fresh aroma of cut grass on which tiny insects are crawling.

The honeybees are humming around the flowers, and their scent is detectable even from a distance. Further away, two-storied brick buildings are gleaming in the sunlight. Bougainvillea, geranium, and petunia flowers are hanging from their balconies. In the play area in the middle of the park, a number of toddlers and children are playing. The parents watch their kids who sit in the designated areas set aside for them.

I have placed the picnic items under the lime tree among whose branches birds' nests can be seen. As I approach the tree, I feel, for an instant, a man's presence. I stand still. I last saw him five years ago. I don't remember his name, and I doubt if he recalls mine. I can't see his face half hidden under that grey straw hat, but I'm sure it's him. Wearing only a short, red pair of trousers, he reclines on the deckchair, sunbathing. He has laid his right hand on that so-called pram.

I can't bear looking at his eagle-eyes. I don't think he has seen me, and even so, I doubt he recognised me.

A strange sort of cold passes through my body. I feel as if my knees are buckling. I'm surprised. Once again, my knees are trembling. I'm shaking all over again. This is really happening. I become anxious again. I touch my face. It's as if I feel, once again, the burning sensation of that slap on my face.

I have often dreamed about this man who, accompanied by his footfalls and the creaking of the wheels of his pram, would get into the bus through its rear door. It's a long time since I've tried to forget all that. By focussing my thoughts on the present and trying to plunge into my humdrum daily affairs, I become less depressed. I've tried not to get caught in that trap for a long time.

'How many times should I tell you I'm hungry?' My son's voice brings me back to myself. I take a deep breath, walk to him, and pick up the bag. My hand freezes half-way through as I pull open the bag's zipper. The man stirs, stretches himself a little, and assumes his defensive attitude again. He draws his pram closer to him. He turns his pale profile towards us, opens his thin lips and says, 'Hi'. Ignoring him, I hand a salami-and-cheese sandwich and fruit juice to my son. His grateful look after biting into the sandwich cheers me up. I'm now certain that at this point in my life, nothing can harm either him or me. I grab his hand and, all of a sudden, kiss his cheek, which is still as soft a young girl's. He frees his hand from mine and runs to children his own age. Last year he learned different types of swimming, and now he is showing off trying to dive into the deeper part of the lake.

I quickly walk back to the quiet spot where I was lying before. I dive into the water and swim among the little black fish to the middle of the lake. The water, filled with calmness and tranquillity, seeps into my body. The water is cooler than I had expected. I swim calmly along the lakeside. I grab the part of the iron ladder in the water and move my feet to get rid of the algae. I feel I love this land. Here is not the land in which I took my first uncertain steps. Here is not my homeland and has no resemblance to it. I feel, however, the safe firmness of the ground beneath my feet. No matter where I've come from, I belong to this land and this sky. My son is still playing on the lakeside. High above, the sun is still shining, and I know it will be sunny all day and night. The croaking of a frog can be heard from the lakeside. The soft rustling of the leaves on the upper branches of the trees caused by the breeze that blows off the lake, mingled with the freshness that penetrates the heart, fills me with joy. I take off the top part of my swimming costume. I now sense the man's heavy stare directed to my body.

It is as if his presence recalls all the days I've been trying to forget. All the rage and dread I've been carrying are lulled into silence. I kept thinking that I would never free myself from this fear, and he belonged to a period of my life to which I would never return. It's still painful when I think about those days. No one pays any attention to me; neither the children who lough loudly and play with their inflatables, the woman who is sunbathing, nor the man who is lying on the lakeside and reading a newspaper. Only the man-with-the-pram is looking at me from a distance. I lie down on my belly and insert my headphones into my ears and listen again to Bob Dylan:

How many times must a man look up
Before he can see the sky?
How many ears must one man have...,

I look at the small waves that repeatedly stick the tiny splinters and dead leaves to the rotten parts of the boardwalk. Finally, a dragonfly with shiny wings hovers backward in a straight line close to my ear. I follow it with half-open eyes. I read somewhere that only dragonflies can fly backward. So, I tell myself, even if it's for once, I must go over everything that has happened to me – to go backward, and start from the beginning until I reach the present! I must try to distance myself from all the moments and events and put the dispersed pieces into a framework with a longer term.

From the first days I saw this man; it was as if my life-story began with him – before and after seeing him, just like the Christian calendar, before and after Christ.

At that time, I was thirty-three. This number, like numbers seven, ten, and twelve, is not only mysterious but also signifies youth and power! I had understood that Jesus was crucified when he was thirty-three.

2

What an unpredictable thing life is. You never know what will happen next. Five years ago, during the first half of my second year in Stockholm, I was leading the life of a helpless immigrant. Winters in Stockholm were different from all the winters I had known. That winter was one of the coldest in a decade.

I lived with my four-year-old son in a tiny room, not unlike that of a nun, in the Täby Municipality. The only furniture in the room was a rickety Ikea bed for one and a half people. Through the only window in the room, one could see an empty nest on top of a leafless plane tree. However, my stay in this cell for one-and-a-half people did not last long. No sooner did my morning sickness, a sure sign of my first months of pregnancy, begin than my landlady found a good excuse to use against me. She was a wrinkled old Polish woman who wound her hair daily in curlers. She decided to evict me just like that.

'Is something happening?' she asked me one morning when I vomited into the toilet for the first time. She followed me to my room and said: 'It was not my intention to let this room to a pregnant woman. Soon I'll have two people living here!'

From Monday to Friday, I took the 611 bus from Erikslund to Danderyd to drop my son in a nursery where a Farsi tutor worked. I returned to Dena Restaurant in the Danderyd and Mörby junction. Without a work permit, I worked in the kitchen of that restaurant.

Just at the next stop where we got on the bus, the man in the park with a pram got on the bus. Showing no willingness to sit, he stood beside his pram until he reached his destination. Holding on to my son's pram, I sat on the first seat in the middle row. He stood so close to his pram that I was able to inhale his scent of soap mixed with cologne. All along the journey, with every jolt of the bus, he kept bending over the pram, tucking in the edges of the blanket under which lay his child.

He was a typical Swedish man. However, there was something peculiar about him. Not wearing a ring on any of his fingers, his hands resembled those of a harp player. I had never seen him with a woman.

I was trying to see the face of the baby in the pram from these modern, chic parts. A healthy baby wrapped in a pure lamb's wool blanket! I always imagined him looking like his father – blue eyes and thin lips. But there was no way to find out. The man would place the pram facing him at all times. I guessed it was because of the severe cold that he covered the baby like that. He wore a pair of corduroy trousers and a thick, woollen jacket.

I was inquisitive in those days. Maybe the mystery surrounding that man and his pram attracted him to me. Flights of fancy sometimes overtake us. I imagined him like me, being a lonely man left with his only child. I fancied we had a lot in common. I kept thinking to myself, perhaps he liked me. The cold, indifferent expression he showed was just the characteristic of the people here. Every day I told myself I must initiate a conversation with him. Often I caught him throwing a furtive glance at me.

I felt he would one day come and sit beside me and start talking to me. Using the pretext of improving my Swedish language, I was looking for an opportunity to talk with him. I could, for example, express my opinion about something. He would then ask me where I came from. I would then tell him from Iran, Iraq or Persia, and I would start talking about me being from the East.

If he stood beside me and turned his head to look at me, I would catch his eyes. My grandmother used to say that my eyes similar to a dog. When I was a child, I did not understand what she meant by that. Only later in my life did I realise what it meant. These eyes are so uniquely fascinating that they can engage those of others as soon as they are fixed on them. I didn't know how to set about knowing someone and keep the friendship going in this country. I didn't know where to begin. Could I start by saying about how cold it was here? Or, tomorrow, it was going to drop to twenty-seven below zero? I could string together some hackneyed clichés such as most of the time, it's sunny in my country, or one could boil an egg in the blistering heat during July.

It was as if I was desperately rummaging among the worn-out layers of my mind to find some things we had in common to talk about before the bus reached its destination.

I kept telling myself that maybe he would invite me for dinner or to go and see a movie. I thought he would sooner or later do that.

My mother used to say to me: 'You live in cloud cuckoo land. You must climb down from the clouds.' But I loved fantasising. I had so often lived on the clouds. I had almost come to wonder if there were any differences between the unreal world of fantasies and the actual one.

I was badly in need of a man. I was dying to talk to someone. Unable to continue, I could not fulfil my dreams without a man.

I thought this man could unravel the tangled skein of my troubled life. In those days, I was a heap of complicated problems. My first and biggest problem was that I had just been denied asylum for the third time by the immigration office. There had not been enough evidence in my application for me to be granted asylum. I received my first rejection after six months. Soon after, the second one followed. Finally, after months of living with dread and anxiety, the third rejection came. This meant that I would have to leave Sweden.

Like a shot in the dark, my only hope of staying here was marriage. It didn't matter who I married, as long as it helped my asylum application.

Afshaar, a middle-aged Iranian man in whose restaurant I worked, had lived in Sweden for years without being a Swedish citizen. Once he had obtained his citizenship, he began to do whatever he could to help his compatriots. He would offer them his assistance without expecting anything from Iranians who would come to ask for his help. He was able to do this thanks to his excellent knowledge of the ins and outs of the laws and regulations of the Immigration office. Over the years, he had set up an establishment similar to that of a clandestine syndicate. His restaurant had turned into a hangout for would-be deported Iranians, the ones who waited for the decisions of the courts run by the Immigration Office, or even those who had recently obtained their citizenship. From time to time, he would either write political articles about these immigrants' human rights, join in demonstrations, or participate in sit-ins.

Most of those who frequented the restaurant, either by joining in the secret gatherings or participating in demonstrations, were losers who openly manifested their streaks of lunacy. On the other hand, however, they sometimes played the saviour, insisting on saving you. Only then would you hear different ways of obtaining permission to remain in Sweden.

'Why don't you tell them you are gay?' one would suggest.

'If you had told them that your husband was a wife-beater and you'd saved your life by running away from him, you'd get your citizenship on the spot,' another would propose.

'Even though I spent years in prisons in Iran and I'd taken with me all the relevant documents, my asylum application was rejected,' another one would say in total despair. No wonder he believed everything depended on luck.

Another one, even after renouncing Islam and converting to Christianity, had been handed his deportation document. He had been told to prove his life would be in danger if he returned to Iran. What hopes would I have had to look into their eyes and tell them that I've come here for my child's sake, to keep him for myself?

'Do you see this lot who have managed to stay here?' Afshaar used to tell me. 'What's interesting and strange about them is that they've come to believe in their lies. After leaving the ball, they've taken part in a masquerade and kept their masks on for such a long time that now the masks are stuck to their faces, having become an integral part of their identity. That's why they're wandering like lost souls in no-man's land. They don't even know if they're political activists chased by someone or other, or whether they're gay. They don't even know exactly if they lived in Iran, and if so, where and how!'

'I've got a brilliant idea,' one of them told me one day. 'Go to Sergel Square and take off all your clothes. Pretend you're protesting against the arrival of the Association of Iranian Economic Executives, which has come to Sweden. Stand in the square holding your son and the Iranian flag in one hand and the other. We'll send off some sympathisers to film you and take some

photos. They'll then give you citizenship on the spot.'
Even thinking of doing such a thing made me tremble.

'Don't you ever listen to their cock-and-bull stories,'
Afshaar would say. 'And don't lose sight of two things:
don't let these people know what you've told the
Immigration Office, and keep the details of your private
life to yourself.'

The most important commandment for Afshaar was
to keep one's asylum case secret.

'They could easily go the Immigration Office and tell
them all sorts of conflicting information about you.
They could recommend your case to others, which
could have unfortunate consequences for you.'

Afshaar considered immigration and applying for
asylum to be an endless nightmare. This was particularly
bad in my case because from the moment I had set foot
in Sweden, the Middle East had been plunged into
infernal conflict giving rise to the flood of immigrants
who headed for Europe. The Immigration Office had
become very meticulous in dealing with numerous
bogus cases.

'In the good old days, the minds of the Swedish folk
were like blank slates,' Afshaar would say. 'It was not as
easy as it is now to access the information about the
asylum-seekers. That's why they readily welcomed the
immigrants. These days the TV and satellite channels

and social media paint grim pictures of the regimes and the people in the Middle-East, making everyone believe that the immigrants are terrorists, rapists, and fraud artists.'

Every morning, while working in Afshaar's pizzeria, I would put the stacked-up chairs and the tables down, and check the fridge with the glass door to make sure it was well-supplied with drinks and let him know. Hung on one of the discoloured walls of the restaurant was an even more faded picture of Damavand Mountain. Whenever the restaurant was not so busy, Afshaar would sit at one of the tables and talk about his political activities in Iran. He had worked for years for the official TV channel of the Islamic Republic. After making a report that got him on the wrong side of the authorities, he was imprisoned in solitary confinement. After undergoing many difficulties, he managed to leave Iran. He would then speak about the day they had gathered in Arlanda Airport and had tried to stop the chartered flight to carry a deported Iranian family back to Iran. He would go on talking about when he sewed his lips together and sat in Sergel Square. Finally, he would end up recounting the time he had gone on a hunger strike for two days after sewing his lips with a thick goblin needle. After this, his lawyer broke the news of his asylum application's success. Arriving at this point of his story, he would look cheerfully victorious, smiling broadly like a man who had won the lottery.

At Afshaar's recommendation, or rather his insistence, I had rented my womb from the first of June to an Iranian couple. The ovum of the woman was planted into my womb. Having had four abortions, her womb could not hold the ovum. Every time the couple tried to conceive a baby, it ended in miscarriage. They insisted that no one should know about this. They chose me because I was a homeless and stateless refugee and was in good physical and psychological health. After two months of our agreement, I was still in shock, wondering why I did this.

'This'll only take nine months,' Afshaar told me one day. 'It'll all pass in the twinkling of an eye.' Then, he whispered in my ear: 'It's impossible for them to deport a pregnant woman.'

Now I had turned into that stork who must deliver the baby wrapped in a white cloth after nine months to that couple's door. I was supposed to pay the deposit for this service to one of Afshaar's customers, who would then be able to arrange a sham marriage for me with an Iraqi man who also spoke Farsi. He had learnt Farsi from the Iranian prisoners of war. He talked proudly about his victories and the killing of the Iranians during the eight-year-old war.

I don't recall much about that war except the continuous warning sirens and our rushing down to damp and dark basements where we waited to hear the Iraqis' missile explosions. Whenever the sounds of the blasts came nearer to our hiding place, my brother would block my ears with his hands and say: 'They're just playing some games, and it'll all be over soon.'

Every time the aerial bombardments were over, I would hear this statement: 'Thank God they did not bomb anywhere near us.' Being so terrifyingly real, these rare occurrences have left their indelible marks on my mind.

Every day after dropping off my son in the nursery, I had to look for a flat to rent. My main problem was that I did not have a certain four-digit number. You are nobody here if you don't possess those cursed four digits. When I say 'nobody', I mean nobody. Even if you wanted to be connected to an operator, you had to spell out your four-digit number. The funny thing about it was that they would, in all probability, ask for it even when you wanted to buy a packet of chewing gum!

I was nothing but an exile without a future. Even if I could speak English, I lost my self-confidence and could not talk to anyone. I was afraid of incorrectly putting my intentions into words. I became like this a long time ago. Whenever I tried to say something, it turned out wrong. The spoken words were opposite to what I had intended. I would then try to put my sentence right, making it sound even worse. I would finally lose track of what I was going to say. Often I found myself in awkward situations, acting clumsily. I then decided to act as dumb as possible, which was not difficult. I knew very well that humans communicate with the outside world only through language. I also knew what would happen to a person if she lost the faculty of speech. I had come to dislike any communication. I started to talk to myself. In our country, they had silenced us in such a way that we had lost the power of speech and instead of speaking, we had learnt to be on our own and hold conversations with ourselves. That meant that we had learnt to live in our shells and not let anyone have access to our feelings.

When the faculty of speech is thwarted, one is only silent. I had been quiet for years. I could also not attend the Swedish language classes for want of that cursed four-digit number.

I was not so enthusiastic about learning Swedish. However, as I worked, I managed to flounder through some words and phrases and understand some of them.

On that particular day in Turkey, a human smuggler called Veronica Pilarsky handed me my counterfeit passport, a fake identity with my photo stuck in it; she told me to tear it up and flush it down the toilet as soon as I passed through the arrivals gate in Sweden. When I questioned her about my going to Sweden, she said: 'You would have more chance of staying in Sweden than anywhere else! So many refugees hope to set foot in Sweden because the moment they arrive, all will be well. Being very kind people, the Swedish will be particularly kind to you as you have a son. Women enjoy many rights there. Do you realise how many refugees would hope to be in your shoes right now? You'll be given a home to live in and a passport with which you can travel to one hundred and seventy countries without applying for visas! Think about Sweden as a launching pad, a platform from which....'

I would never have thought I would end up here. I remember the geography lessons for all the school years were compulsory. The Department of Education distributed the textbooks and all the students of a particular year had to study the same lessons, including Religious and Koranic education. My father used to say: 'Why do they shove this nonsense down our kids' throats? This is a kind of brainwashing!'

The majority of the Iranians were Muslims at that time, as a large number of Christians and Jews had left Iran at the first opportunity. We belonged to those Jews who could not go and had to conceal their identity. Our friends advised us that we should never talk about how we lived our private lives. This absolute secrecy had become second nature to those Jews who had stayed behind from the moment they could tell right from wrong. My mother was a headteacher and never managed to accept the ruling system. I found out later on that she had leftist tendencies. She had hidden in the home lots of books by Lenin, Stalin, and books such as the Brothers Karamazov. We were often asked in the school questions such as: 'Do you have any books at home? What are their titles? Do you have alcoholic drinks at home? Does your father listen to foreign radio? Do you have videos at home?' In those years, it was a crime to have videos, cassettes, or books other than religious ones or books about the Koran. I never understood why my father watched Charles Bronson, and Costa-Gavras films or my brother sat in the dark and watched 'The Wall' by Pink Floyd. If the regime detected the slightest indication of Jewishness in some people, they would be in danger of heavy penal accusations such as spying for Israel. The consequences of such charges could range from torture to death. Iran had always been and still is, the land of paradoxes.

One day they decided to expel me from my school because I had rubbed off my classmate's phrase under her drawing that said 'Death to America' and wrote on it instead, 'Death to Khomeini'. She was one of those girls who always pulled her hijab up to her chin. I had come to believe that America belonged to my paternal relatives as all of them except my father and my grandfather lived in America.

What I did that day could end up in my exclusion from the school or perhaps in my father's arrest or imprisonment. My father came to the school and convinced them, with his customary sweet-talk, that the phrase was only a spelling mistake, accusing me of being giddy and scatterbrained. Hearing this, the headteacher was convinced that I was a bit foolish. I was a little distracted, constantly losing my belongings at school. My brother would tease me by saying: 'Surprised you didn't lose yourself today!' Sometimes I would take off my hijab in the classroom and lose it. I would be punished for this by being forced to stand in the corner of the school.

I knew that I would face a heavy punishment home, where I hid in my brother's room while he was talking to my father outside the room.

'Don't worry,' my brother said upon entering the room. 'You haven't done anything wrong. You've only written down what you think is right, that's all.'

Later on, he would recount this incident to his friends with a smile, saying: 'She's not a child. She's a brave rebel.' After that, I did my best not to be near my father for long.

When I was in the fourth year of primary school, we learned what Sweden looked like on the map and also its capital's location in geography lessons. We had to remember that Sweden was in the continent of Europe and is near the North Pole and that half of the year there is daylight and the other is darkness. I recall now I found it odd to have sunlight for one half of the year and night for the other half! I would never have thought I would end up here.

Those days I was busy trying to obtain American residency to go to the Promised Land. All I hoped for was to go there because my paternal relatives lived in the United States. I focused on that goal, and nothing was able to change my determination. I invested whatever I had in reaching this goal. Despite everything being topsy-turvy, I made a firm resolve to leave. I knew full well that I had to pull my chestnuts out of the fire. I, however, had no clear picture in my mind about my future or my son's.

So many plans were whirling non-stop inside my head in a chaotic fashion. Besides, I wanted to find out if I was woman enough to face up to the challenge. Now that I was in Sweden, there was no going back. I was determined to fight to the finish.

Knowing full well that it was a futile, repetitive task, I would contact humanitarian organisations every week or call the Red Cross to seek advice. Finally, after listening to me attentively, they promised to follow my case through their channels. But nothing ever happened.

The problem was that I had arrived in Sweden at the wrong time. The Middle-East had been plunged into chaos. The flood of immigrants who had come to Europe, the Syrian civil war, the invasion of hundreds of thousands of refugees, and the *Allah-o akbar*-chanting terrorists who attacked people indiscriminately had all-in-all, contributed to the opposing views held by the Swedish authorities towards the foreigners. Not being European makes you feel like an outsider with frustrated hopes. Since I arrived in this country, I have tried to stand on my own two feet. It was as if I wanted to tell them I was not an economic migrant who had come here to steal the bread and butter from their table. The worst part of it all was that you were invisible here!

Every day the bus would stop at the right hour on the dot, and I saw the man waiting outside on the pavement. He would push the door button outside the bus, get on with his pram, and throw a furtive glance at me. I had often caught his eyes looking at me. He would quietly and cautiously bend over the pram, looking at it attentively.

However hard I tried to see the face of the child under the blanket, I failed. With incredible perseverance, he would carefully tuck the child in. Some days I wanted to tell him that the baby would be stifled under the blanket.

I was becoming heavier by the day, the opposite of when I was pregnant with Danial because I now looked as thin as a rake. The day my mother threw a *viaraaneh* party for me and invited all the neighbours and women relatives to have all kinds of Iranian and foreign foods, none of them could believe I was four-months pregnant. It is a tradition in Iran that the pregnant woman's mother should prepare a *viaraaneh* and invite everyone. Viaraaneh means all the foods that the pregnant woman craves.

'Eat these foods; otherwise, your boy's willy will be circumcised,' my mother said at the party.

I grew bigger every day then, even though I ate so little. It was as if my body knew that this fertilised ovum was not mine and was reacting to it. I had come here with a half-empty suitcase and a child in much worse health than I was. Now I was carrying a foetus fluttering like a butterfly in my belly. I kept asking myself why I had been a carrier all my life. Now I had to carry the heaviest burden on my shoulders – myself. You would have thought I had always been a carrier of my lost beliefs, assumptions, and the injuries inflicted on my soul. I had accepted the pain of eternally carrying these loads without knowing my destination. Yet, my instinct told me that this man was also a carrier.

That day it was twenty below, and the cold was freezing our bones. Early morning Afshaar called me to tell me he had received a letter after I left the restaurant from the police station saying that the Immigration Office had passed on my documents to Police Head Office to deal with. That meant that they could arrest me at any minute. After telling me this news, he reassured me that I should not be worried; he had seen a skilful solicitor who had promised to deal with my case. He then said that although the Immigration Office is meticulous, it sometimes makes unusual mistakes. He reassured me again by saying: 'Don't worry!'

Wanting to go to the nursery, Danial had cried in the morning, but I had to talk to Afshaar. It was the end of November, and I still had not found a place to live.

I saw the man who got on the bus and stood in his usual place. The bus was warm, and Danial pulled the hood of his anorak off after constantly fiddling with it. The man wore the same check jacket, over which he wore a grey overcoat with a red scarf round his neck, and was standing there as impassive as ever. As the bus jolted along, his coat moved. I could not see his eyes as he was looking the other way. From the moment he got on the bus, I could see that he was agitated. I stroked my belly as I felt pain in my groin. It would be impossible for him to see my bulging belly under a heap of clothes in which I was wrapped to keep warm. Even if he did find out, I could explain that I was not with anyone and tell him that the baby in my belly was the result of a sort of Immaculate Conception like the Virgin Mary, who was conceived in an outpatient job without any man touching me. My mother kept badgering me about why I had not sent a photo of myself and Danial for a while. I had no idea what to do with my puffy eyes and swollen lips. Looking at my photos, she would understand what had happened. How could I then explain everything to her? 'Yes, mother, I've rented my womb to someone so that the Immigration Office is confronted with a done deal so that I'll not be put in an aeroplane and sent back to that damned place.'

Danial loved collecting small toys given free of charge to kids at MacDonald's. He always kept a few of those toys in his pram. He cried the whole morning that day. The heat in the bus made him so frustrated that he suddenly threw out the toy in an angry outburst. The toy landed in the man's pram immediately after Danial cried. Having found the opportunity I was waiting for, I got up at once, bent over the pram, and slipped my hand under the blanket in such a way as to fetch the toy and find out about the nature of that mysterious pram. Perhaps I could use this as an excuse to strike up a friendship with the man. My hand remained motionless under the blanket, not because I was waiting to give the man time to say something to me but because there was nothing under the blanket - no baby. No sooner had I turned my questioning eyes to the man when he raised his hand and struck me in the face. The power of the strike shocked me so severely that, for a moment, I felt something extraordinary had happened. Feeling hot and stunned, the whole experience and the man's reaction did not sink in. I recovered from the shock only because my face was stinging so much. Thinking that everybody was staring at me, I felt ill at ease. At this moment, the bus stopped with a jolt. Looking as cold as the icy air of the town, the passengers got off silently through the door in the middle of the bus. Without uttering a word or a glance at me that showed his regret, the man was the last to get off.

Overcome by rage, the thought of pushing him off the bus or killing him flashed through my mind. I gazed at the nape of his neck and then at my own hands. After everyone left the bus, I grabbed Danial's hand, pushed his pram out, and got off. The bus had stopped at the Dendrid Station near the entrance to the underground. I didn't feel the shock of this dreadful experience as I stood. You don't feel the effect of something horrible happening to you standing among a group of people.

Feeling nauseous, I could hear the thumping of my heart. All of a sudden, I felt a lump in my throat – a lump that stifled all my fears, frustrations, and the insults made to me in the course of my life. I burst into tears. Hearing me cry, the people, who had descended the bus, turned unexpectedly and hurried towards me like grains of wheat pouring out of a drum. Circling me, they sympathised with me. Crying loudly, I put my arm on my eyes as I used to do when I was a child.

The icy wind was cutting my face like sharp razors. After winding around my knees, it lashed them and cut my armpits like a dagger. Danial kept looking at my hot tears that were turned into a vapour after dropping on the melted snow under my feet. He had bent over and was trying to look up at my face. For a long time, he had never seen me cry like that. I cried even louder after catching him looking at me. I choked so much of my heart and soul into that crying. I had not sobbed like that since my childhood.

This was not the first slap on the face in my life. But I was sure that this would be the worst and last insult I ever had from the people of this unfamiliar country.

3

The library door was kicked off its hinges. I don't recall how many or where they sprung from. I could never tell whether it was the sound of their feet or the noise of the slammed door. The whole thing happened so suddenly that I felt my heart miss a beat. A few men with mop-like hair and bushy beards were slapping my face and pulling my arms. I felt my head joining something other than my neck. Some unfamiliar faces were bending over me.

As they pushed me around, hitting me all over my body with the butts of their guns, I kept instinctively hugging my knees to protect myself from the violent blows. I fell on my face and gashed my forehead. A warm pool of blood spread on the floor. I felt like each impact was tearing off a small piece of my body. I tried to get up after I was pushed down the stairs. The blasts of shotguns mingled with screams could be heard everywhere. Blood had trickled down my face, onto my hands, and to the soles of my feet. I was unable to stand on my feet. Where were the screams coming from? Where was the door of this room through which the noises were coming?

I fell flat on my face on the cold floor. Everywhere smelt of gunpowder and dust. The floor tiles of the university dormitory were spattered with blood – the warm blood of the students sprawled on the library floor. I wanted to say something but couldn't as my mouth was filled with blood.

Someone was yelling into my ear: 'You mother-fuckers! We didn't make a revolution so that a whole lot of scumbags, nancy boys, and whores could come along and do whatever they wanted. Where do you think this place is? You lily-livered arseholes are full of shit. We'll teach you a lesson that you'll never forget!'

One Basiji was straddling my back and saying, 'I haven't fucked a whore for seven years! Once we are at the centre, I'll tell you what I'll do with you!'

He was right. We didn't understand. We didn't get that we didn't have the right to express our opinions here. We didn't comprehend that we didn't belong to this country. It was theirs! I was struck with the first blow of a truncheon at the back of my knee, forcing me to fall flat on my face. My sight became blurry.

There was a great clamour of voices. We thought we were all going to die there. Someone was shouting: 'Escape!' Not knowing where to go, we started to run. We looked like a flock of people making a dash towards the university's main entrance. It was as if a pack of wolves had set upon a flock of sheep. The men were as vast and strange-looking as Neanderthals.

'Run, Nina!' Isaac shouted at me. I couldn't open my eyes. He threw himself on me. The truncheon blows were now raining on my head. Lying there, I drew my knees to my chest just like that day when he sat in a taxi, rubbing himself against me.

With his scruffy hair, he was one of the funniest students at the university. He was full of vitality and cheer. The first time I saw him was in a philosophy lecture. That day the topic for discussion was postmodernist philosophy that, as the lecturer was expounding, had been influenced by existentialism and phenomenology. He went on to talk about its origins and avant-garde philosophy. Once, he began to speak about Jean-Paul Sartre by reciting his famous saying, 'Our choices are like the birds who take to flight from the earth.' Isaac raised his hand and said: 'Why can't other human beings influence our choices?' He and the lecturer went on discussing for a while. Isaac was trying somehow to lead us to the point that our moral choices must have sources other than human beings. I had almost figured out that he was a traditionalist, not an intellectual. Now I realise that he always liked confrontation. Having always shaky and precarious notions about the meaning of words, he had tangled himself in traditional ideas. According to him, everyone should regress. I liked listening to him using big words. Everybody said that he was very clever and the best. One of the books he always had with him was 'Understanding Derrida'.

Both of us being enthusiastic, we thought the future would hold lots of hidden promises for us. With our youth's feverish eyes, we saw the future as something mysterious that would reveal its secrets to us even if a cloak was spread over it. We were cocksure, however, that our future would be bright and full of success. Isaac was studying philosophy and sociology. Both of us were thinking of building the future of our homeland.

'All the Iranians should study philosophy to stop them from being shallow thinkers,' he kept saying. 'We must think. Only thinking can make society better.'

He was a few months younger than me. At the begining of our friendship, he had asked me to marry him. I told him that I had other goals to think about. I never told him that I had feelings for him.

There were always a handful of students like him at the university. He was an intelligent, popular, kind, and sharp-eyed boy. One could tell this from the glint in his eyes. It was as if he had a mutant gene, was far ahead of his time and knew about everything. He had a strong interest in current affairs. You would have thought he was a custodian of thousands of years of knowledge. No one, however, is perfect. Being a single child, he was spoilt.

Coming from a traditional and very religious family, Isaac was trying to show that he was against tradition. There was, of course, something more to him. He was incapable of ridding himself of the religious and moral traditions that his people had inculcated in his head since childhood. He believed that people must do one thousand things to achieve their goals. I acted in those days as if I was bewitched and gagged.

'Witchcraft and casting spells on people has been going on since olden times, love,' my grandmother used to say. 'The world goes round according to laws that no one can make sense of. People do so many things to get what they want. There are one thousand ways you know nothing about and can't see. So say "No" and finish the job!'

But I was scared. I mean, I was always afraid. Now I was even more fearful of the future – of ending up in prison, of the horrible things they did to my friends, of being raped, of mass graves, of being wiped off the face of the earth, or such like! After the siege of the university, the butchering, the killing, the arresting, and the imprisonment of the students, most of the lectures had been cancelled. The university had been turned into ruins. Only a small number had been able to return to their lessons. During the onslaught on the students in the university precinct, so many of them had been killed, and even more had gone missing. The corpses of so many of the dead had vanished from the face of the earth. Their families were neither able to protest nor were able to search for their loved ones. They were not even allowed to mourn the dead freely. They kept their weeping, their protests, and their mourning to themselves. It was reported in the national newspapers that no one had been killed during the attack except several foreign provocateurs who were disguised as students, and they were all arrested!

After that incident, I was expelled from the university. I soon realised that all my efforts had gone to ruin. I had no document to prove that I had studied there for four years. One day I woke up and realised that all was lost. Having lost heart, I felt that everything had turned to rust. The days came and went, and I was left helpless, unable to do anything.

No one knew why they had begun to crush the students like that! In those days of the reign of terror, they were looking for scapegoats, and we, the educated and enlightened layer of the society happened to be close at hand. This was sufficient to suppress the whole community. The regime had set in motion a crushing, stupid, and hideous political trickery on its people.

They had wreaked havoc on the books in the university library. All the lectures were held under the watchful eyes of the Revolutionary Guards. Most of the lectures had been cancelled. I had been overcome with an ominous sense of foreboding. I was not even allowed to enter the university grounds.

'You haven't lost anything,' Isaac kept telling me. 'The degrees here are nothing but worthless pieces of paper.'

I soon realised I had nothing to do with that society. So how could I return to society and start my relationships, friendships, and business affairs all over again? A dark, sinister veil enveloped everything. I was bogged down in a mire of misunderstandings, uncertainties, compromises, and bungle after bungle.

When Isaac and I went to the cemetery, we found it filled with our university classmates. He kept weeping even for those whom he did not recognise. He stood beside all the graves and stared numbly at the pictures of the dead young men that gazed at us.

'We have given our blood,' he said. 'Do you understand what it means? We must not let their blood be wasted.'

It was as if that day, a powerful storm had raised all the dust and dirt that settled on this land throughout its troubled history and turned it into a big lump in Isaac's throat. It looked as if you had come to a macabre party held by the mothers of the dead. These grotesquely disfigured-looking mothers were offering people votive dates, halva, and fruit juice. Covered from head to foot in black veils, they talked to one another in hushed voices. However much I searched, I couldn't find a picture of a young woman on any tombstone. Isaac constantly had a lump in his throat, with his face distorted, just like a two-year-old boy when they became upset. He kept gazing at one picture and then moving to another one.

I talked so much that I ended up not listening to him. But, like a child, his curiosity was thousands times more than mine. He wanted to get to know other people and understand the sorrows of the folk with whom he came into contact. He was a true revolutionary who participated in all the revolutionary committee's activities. All the time, he talked about political matters.

I was not a political person; I was not affiliate with any political party.

After the university incident, he again asked me to marry him. He had promised to provide me with an ordinary and hassle-free life. He was willing to do anything to marry me. He wanted to pay a formal visit to our house with his family to ask for my hand in marriage.

'It is our natural right to find our other half in life,' he used to say. 'Only a traditional marriage would ensure the continuation of our union.'

Having had a martyred brother, Isaac strongly believed in custom and tradition. Being so restless, he always wanted to do something. Being left with no other choice, I finally agreed to marry him. I accepted his conditions without even questioning them. He had arguments with his family for a long time and threatened to abandon them for good. My parents were also shocked when I broke the news of the marriage proposal. My father believed that this would be like a shameful stain on our relatives and ancestors.

I, however, had made up my mind. I had locked myself up in my room. I used to do this when I was a child.

'Come on out and have your dinner,' my father would say. 'Your stomach has nothing to do with this!'

I had decided to insist so much that they would give in. This was a sort of hunger strike!

Isaac would buy clothes and jewellery for me, anything I wanted. Every time he bought something new for me, I never asked him where he got the money for such expensive things. I knew that he got that sort of money from his father.

At that time of my life, I needed someone to look after me, someone who would lift me and hold me tight. All this was due to my insecurity, and Isaac was the only one there for me. I felt I owed him a debt of gratitude as long as I lived. Had he not been there, I would have stayed in prison for years.

We got married amid assassinations and arrests. He promised me he would not get involved in politics as long as he lived. He often said fighting for freedom and social justice and empathising with the sorrows of others does not necessarily mean one is political. According to him, if someone does not care about the freedom of human beings, the pain of others does not upset him. On the other hand, if he does not think of ways of reducing the suffering of others, then he is not a human being.

We lived in a backward and rotten society – an archaic society whose leader was a hideous, depraved old hyena. It had been a long time since the life of the leader of this decrepit society had come to an end. They were both on their last legs. Without telling me, Isaac had become the leader of the same organisation he used to be a member of. In those days, suppression was reigning monstrously supreme. The regime's clampdown on people was so oppressive that they nipped any dissenting voice in the bud. The moment there was a protest gathering, the regime's supporters would either run over the protesters or throw them from the bridges, or in the dead of night, they would land like those alien spaceships in a district and abduct the marked ones.

'Let's both of us leave Iran and join my uncles in America,' I kept telling Isaac during those days. 'After selling the house, we can leave.'

'What house?' he would answer. 'My father has bought this house for me. I'll never sell this house as long as I'm alive. Besides, don't lose sight that I'm the only son left for them.'

He would never listen to me. Maybe our lot would have been better if he was not a spoiled brat. Finally, my father came to my room the day I was about to go to the synagogue.

'I've got a few words to tell you,' he said calmly. 'Are you ready to hear them?'

I knew that he would go on about things I was familiar with.

'From the moment you say "Yes" to this marriage,' he went on, 'do you realise what rights you'll have to relinquish? Do you realise you'll have to give up everything you hold dear? Do you realise that you'll never be able to travel alone after signing the marriage contract? That you will never have the right of child custody? That you cannot go to work without your husband's permission? That you cannot continue your education without his permission? He'll decide where and in which city you'll live. I hope you understand all this! Ponder all this and be aware of what you're getting yourself into!'

I didn't want to listen to him. I was fed up with his advice. So when I started my new life in Isaac's home, I only had one thing in mind – to abandon everything, distance myself from the past and focus on my married life and what I wanted to be and to do. It was not a difficult task to achieve. Then, following my feminine instincts, I could play the role of the domestic goddess in my new home.

In the first days of our marriage, whenever I rolled over in our bed and woke up with a start in the middle of the night, I would remain silent and dazed for a moment. It would take a few seconds before I found out what time of day it was, where I was, and who was that man sleeping beside me. Then, the moonlight would slowly pour into the room through the net curtains and fall on Isaac's face with his thick hair, broad forehead, bushy black eyebrows, aquiline nose, and prominent cheekbones, and would put me in mind of those faces on Achaemenid friezes. Our framed picture of our wedding day on the wall would then emerge in the pale light.

I scattered perfume bottles, cologne bottles, and lipsticks on my dressing table. The floor around the bed was strewn with Isaac's clothes. I would promise myself that I would wake up and prepare breakfast for the groom to welcome the daylight. This I never did. I would fall asleep again, only to see that the groom had picked up his clothes and left the house after buying fresh bread and preparing the tea for me. I would get up and promise to make his breakfast the day after. This would not happen yet again. Most days, I kept myself occupied with reading. Just before sundown, I would remember that I had to prepare supper. I would sit down with the cookbook in my hand and get so absorbed in reading that the smell of burnt meat and onion filled the house so many times that Isaac's parents, who lived on the floor below us, could smell it. Isaac's mother would, most of the time, come up without warning and begin to moan about how wretched her son was and so on. Once she left, I would resume my reading. I had read all the books on Isaac's bookshelves. I had started buying books from the bookshops.

Isaac always returned home carrying some shopping which he did himself. On the way home with his father, he bought whatever we needed from the bazaar. He would help me set the table and would place the dishes in the dishwasher after supper. He whistled and sang as he worked. He would often kiss me, saying: 'I was looking for you in heaven and found you here on earth.' I was sad that I didn't know how to be kind towards him and that I was not a suitable bride. I felt regretful for thinking about being a free woman and living away from his parents. I wanted to make up for his kindness.

Early every morning, Isaac would leave the house and return home after nightfall. Following his interests, he worked hard to achieve his goals. Having resigned myself to this kind of life, I perhaps even felt contented. I kept on buying things I did not need. I was not allowed to find a job. According to Isaac's father, we had sufficient money to get by and it went against the family's social standing for their only daughter-in-law to work. When I look back now, I realise there was not a single occasion on which I had to decide. All day long, I would yawn and read books whose titles I had heard of before: In Search of Lost Time, The Brothers

Karamazov, A Soul Enchanted, War and Peace, Anna Karenina..., psychology books and sometimes self-discovery. I read any book I could put my hand on. Occasionally I read romantic fiction and entertaining books that help me identify with the main love-smitten protagonist. These books helped me while away my days. Besides, under those circumstances, the best thing I could do was to keep out of sight, putter about, and daydream.

Every day, I would peep through the cookbook and make some very spicy dishes – one day, a Thai dish; another day, an Indian one with hot spices. Some days I would spend hours lovingly dusting the picture-frames, decorative knick-knacks, the vases, and even the petals of the flowers. I would visit the shops to buy bedspreads with velvety, flowery patterns. I would go to the hairdresser to have my eyebrows done. I would entertain the women and girls of my relatives in my home. I was so idle that I wished to give birth to a dozen children. This kind of life carried on for nearly two years when one day, I told Isaac that I was pregnant.

When I was pregnant with Danial, I spent hours in the house familiarising myself with the objects I had bought for my child. Whatever I bought, I kept showing them to my child in my belly. But, unfortunately, Isaac was only interested in following the news and talking about international affairs.

The birth of my child kept me so preoccupied that I thought of nothing but him. All of a sudden, life had become sweet and free of problems. I had brought a boy into this world. My mother-in-law fainted in the hospital after seeing my son. Everyone was saying that Danial had been born again! My son looked exactly like his martyred uncle, who was called Danial. My son also had a mole behind his ear to complete the resemblance, just like his uncle. Isaac's mother believed that her son was reincarnated into his son's body. For this reason, they named my son 'Danial' without asking my opinion.

A sense of wonder struck me. Lost in amazement, I would keep looking at Danial. My mother-in-law kept swooning over him all the time. As for Isaac, he had become settled in his ways, pursuing his goals instead of paying much attention to us. When someone has a purpose, he achieves it in a calm and composed fashion without trying to persuade others vehemently. I realised that he would never give up on what interested him.

I remember that day very well – a public holiday around the beginning of April. Wearing a white tracksuit and a green muffler, Isaac was ready to leave the house. We had stopped talking long ago about what used to interest us both. All our talks were now about Danial and his needs or what to buy for the house. With our limited communication, the atmosphere in the home was becoming stifling, particularly with the piling up of my unhappiness with Isaac and his family! I was feeling anxious. I knew I had had bad dreams the night before, the contents of which I couldn't remember. I grabbed his hand and asked him not to go. He bent over me and kissed the nape of my neck. Without uttering a word, I kissed his forehead and his eyes and said: 'Please, don't go!' No sooner had he shut the house door than I opened it. The whole of the lane was bathing in the sunlight. He turned and looked at me. With bright eyes, he looked me all over except my face. Looking troubled and restless, he seemed to want to say something to me. Deciding not to say anything, he beckoned me to return to the house and was gone. His eyes shone with excitement and mischief. Looking like a horizon set on fire, his eyes' irises had turned golden-brown under the sun. I knew he was as animated as any of the people in the streets of Tehran!

The following week Danial was going to be two yours old. Every morning I made a liquid food made of almond powder and sugar and a boiled egg for Danial. Isaac had made a little play area in front of the telly for Danial. I left him in his play area to watch his favourite programme, 'Granny Einstein'. The sunlight had fallen onto the middle of the handwoven silk rug in the drawing room. As I busied myself with the ingredients that Isaac had bought to prepare lunch, I could hear Danial chucking his toys around in the drawing room.

The entire morning I had tried not to be worried. No longer able to wait, I called his mobile. He didn't answer. After trying again, he still didn't reply to my call. I left a message for him.

Not hearing from him until well after midnight, I began to feel perturbed. I had left more than twenty messages for him, all of which were left unanswered. I was now more angry than anxious. Then, two plain-clothes agents knocked on our door early the following day. I thought they had come to tell me the news of Isaac's death, which they had to do, anyway. On second thought, I blamed myself for jumping to this hasty conclusion. I had hardly covered my head with my scarf when they kicked the door in with their boots.

I will never forget the moment when the agents entered the house. They forced their way in without showing me any warrant or court order. There were two thickly-bearded men followed by a woman veiled in a *chador*!

Danial was fast asleep. Without caring that a child was sleeping in the bedroom, they switched on the lights and began to turn everything upside down in the house. One of them put the laptop under his arm. I phoned my father and asked him to come over quickly. The woman approached me, snatched the receiver from me and whacked me hard. Completely stunned, I kept stammering asking what was going on.

Having endured all that, I knew there would be more bad news. Having woken up, Danial kept crying, looking for his bottle. I lifted him and hid in the kitchen. I had to wait until my father came. The woman came and stood beside me like a commando. I felt stupid and humiliated. It felt like she was accusing me of something I had no knowledge of. The door of the house was opened, and my parents walked in. I became more frightened seeing their terror-stricken looks. My father looked at me as if he was saying: 'You deserve it.' I desperately wanted to tell him I had done nothing wrong.

The woman shoved me into the van and sat beside me. They then blindfolded me. I heard the van's door slam behind me, followed by Danial's crying and screaming.

***

I found myself in a room when they took the blindfold off. The same woman who came to our house, accompanied by a man who introduced himself as the interrogator, walked in through the room's open door.

I did not make head or tail of the questions they asked me. 'You'll confess after some good beating that'll make you feel better,' the woman screeched after spitting on my face.

But I had nothing to confess! Nothing! I was looking for Isaac's eyes in the darkness populated with black-clothed phantoms. I kept retching, and that filled my mouth with a bitter taste. I was constantly crying and going to the toilet to vomit. I missed Danial and Isaac. I kept telling them I had to go home. I wanted my child to smell his body, to put him to sleep by singing a lullaby for him, and to hold his head against my breast.

I don't know after how many months, as I had become so numb and confused that I had lost count of time, I was freed after Isaac's father pawned the title deed of his house. But, as I was accused of waging war against the Islamic Republic, my sentence had to be carried out before they set me free. Handcuffed and with my feet in chains, they took photos of me, as if I were a criminal, in the corridor of the office of the public prosecutor. Then, after taking my fingerprints, they sent me to the women's section, where I could easily see the quarantine where they kept the prisoners condemned to death by hanging. I still had not fathomed the profundity of the catastrophe that had befallen me until a middle-aged, bulky woman, accompanied by a younger one, entered the room.

'What crime have you committed?' the large woman asked.

I had scarcely opened my mouth to answer when the younger one ordered: 'Take your clothes off!'

'Why should I take off my clothes?' I croaked inaudibly.

'Sit down now stark naked on the chair!' the middle-aged one cawed.

When I straddled the chair, I could see the thick leather lash in her hand from the corner of my eye. I said to myself this must surely be a show. Why was this happening? I had done nothing wrong.

'The sentence must be carried out,' she said. 'The more you shriek, the more lashes there will be. This is what the law says!'

'She won't lash me hard,' I said to myself. 'They're only doing this to scare me.' After being lashed several times, the cold sweat trickled down my back, burning the marks left by the lashes. I could hardly breathe while my breath was burning my nostrils.

***

Outside the Evin Prison, I saw Danial sleeping in the back seat of Isaac's father's car. My father and Isaac's father, with puffed-up eyes and wearing black, were waiting for me outside the iron gate of the prison. I couldn't bear looking into my father's blaming look. Once in the car, I couldn't lean back. I tried to hug Danial, but my mother said: 'Let him be. He's sleeping!'

Everything seemed unfamiliar to me, like an outsider who had found himself lost in a foreign city. I began to retch again. Everything made me feel sick. I thought to myself I was being humiliated all over again. But, more than anything else, I felt tense and irritable. I asked them to drive me to my mother's home. I needed to retreat to my room, close the windows, hug Danial, and think of nothing. My brain had stopped working.

Everyone was sunk into deathly silence in the car that stopped later in front of Isaac's father's house. Isaac had been killed, and his corpse was never returned to us. I don't know why I was not upset about this calamity that had befallen me. Isaac was my son's father, and I failed to comprehend my apathy. Not knowing what I should do after this, I felt, above all, disturbed.

'You must come and stay with us,' my father-in-law said after pulling on the handbrake.

'You're our daughter-in-law, and now you're like our daughter who reminds us of our lost son.' He then pointed at Danial and said: 'And he reminds me of my martyred son!'

'Every individual has a limited tolerance for pain and sorrow,' my grandmother used to say. One has a low tolerance for them, and another has a high one. When you reach the end of your rope, you'll be filled to the brim.'

Maybe after those horrible experiences, I had decided to remain silent by denying the exact nature of the conspiracy that had brought me to this juncture. Sometimes I imagined that Isaac's father had a role in all that. So in the Immigration Office, which resembled the interrogation office in my own country, I didn't talk about how my family treated me. I only told them I had come to Sweden for my son's sake, like how Meursault, the main protagonist in 'The Outsider' of Albert Camus, replied to the Public Prosecutor.

I was not ready to tell them my story from the begining. I just told them my husband had died, and my father-in-law wanted to take my son away from me. I didn't even have a document to prove my identity. How could I put together a document under those circumstances? Neither could I go back very far in time. That's why I began to tell the story from where, after months of living as a widow-in-black in my father-in-law's house, one night, I grabbed my child and without telling anyone, I escaped from Iran. Unable to think, I unconsciously kept dilly-dallying to end my sentences meaningfully. I felt my soul had been injured. When you cannot talk to anyone about certain things in your life, the distance between you and them grows longer and longer.

It was as if my life had been cleaved into two parts. Now all those memories were finding their way bit by bit into my mind. Having done so, they assumed real and frightening forms, becoming tangible and free-from-defect. They were not hallucinations that would break up and scatter about like clouds. Neither were they figments of my imagination to be lost in the hidden recesses of my mind. They were part and parcel of my being that existed and were real. Being a treasure-house of original Iranian sayings and proverbs, my grandmother was an extraordinary woman. You would think she carried in her person thousands of years of traditions. She was not an educated woman, but she was more knowledgeable than any other educated person I'd ever encountered. After giving birth to a brood of five children, of whom my father was the eldest, she had become widowed at the age of thirty, after which she had never remarried. She always enjoyed talking about sacrificing so much to raise her children.

'I carried them around between my teeth and sent them all to university,' she would say.

Hearing her say this, I couldn't help but imagine a cat carrying her kittens in her mouth. They had all gone to America except my father, who looked after her. One day, towards the end of her life, she said she wanted to see her children in America. Being an old Jewish woman, she quickly got her visa. Towards the end of her life, she had become plagued with a strange sort of forgetfulness. In my paternal aunt's house in New Jersey, where she stayed, my grandmother had gotten into the habit of throwing my aunt's jewellery out of the window. During her stay in my uncle's house, she cut the hand-woven silk carpet with traditional Iranian motifs into pieces with scissors. I knew that she had done all this on purpose. This unkind behaviour was an unconscious reaction she was showing to her children. Perhaps this was just a kind of dramatic anger. She also had done some weird things that made my relatives decide to put her in a nursing home in America. It was there that someone pushed her down the stairs. She broke her hip after this accident, became bedridden, and soon passed away.

'You uncles are incapable of looking after people,' my father used to say. I remembered the border controls officer looking suspiciously at my invalid passport photo. The photo was not valid for me to leave the country. My father-in-law had kept my birth certificate, which was as useless as all my other certificates. My national diploma, my university entrance exam, the proof of my years in the university, my marriage certificate, my child's birth-certificate, and my husband's death-certificate were all of no use to me at all. What service could such an identity have for me? One could live without an identity in this country, without a card on which your photo was stuck. When I went to the General Registry Office to let them know that I had lost my birth-certificate and apply for a duplicate copy for Danial, the man behind the counter cast a suspicious glance at me and said: 'We need the signature of your child's guardian in the presence of a solicitor. Otherwise, we can't provide it for you.' He then asked me: 'Where's your birth-certificate, madam? How do we know that you're married?'

'He's dead,' I said calmly.

'Where's this child's guardian?'

'I'm his guardian.'

'No. You're not regarded as his guardian. His father's father can be his guardian. Or, you must obtain a formal document from the court that gives you a power of attorney.'

I lingered so much that the man picked up his pen and said: 'Go with your child's guardian to the notary public office so that you can obtain a duplicate copy of your birth-certificate.'

The thing is that I was unable to obtain even a birth-certificate for my son. Not only was I nobody in my homeland, but also I didn't have anyone here. I had no document to prove who I was. I was suffering from Ulysses Syndrome. You would have thought it had been my lot to be driven out of my homeland. Even after emigrating, all I was left with was daily stress and anxiety.

I was scared of this different, unfamiliar, uncertain and terrible world full of pit-holes. Ulysses was the mythological Greek hero king of a little island. It took him ten years to return to his home after the war with Troy finished. He was the one when the monster Calypso asked his name he replied: 'My name is nobody!'

I was truly a 'nobody' in Sweden. I felt the ground giving way under my feet. Now I had to think of making this place my home. Where is 'home', and what does it mean, anyway?

4

To find a home here in Sweden was a complicated business as there were no such things as estate agents. Although there were websites with only emails that advertised houses and flats for letting, some never replied to my enquiries when I emailed them. Maybe they announced some apartments to allure people to the place to get a deposit from them. I got a few responses by email and wearing the best dress I had, I visited the area only to be told they needed to see my residency permit. They would then ask me if I had a national card or a permanent job. On some occasions, I forestalled them by telling them I would be prepared to pay the whole year's rent. This ploy had an even more damaging effect.

Hooshyaar, the man who was supposed to be my husband in a sham marriage, found a flat for me on top of a Mekonom mechanics workshop situated in one of the side boulevards in the Täby district. He worked as a mechanic in the workshop. Most of the time, his job was to change the winter tyres to summer ones and vice versa! The flat had a kitchen, a small sitting room, and an old, ghastly-looking bedroom. All the doors and the walls were covered with holes left from nails that the other tenants had used. It was one of those flats that smelled of men who had stayed there to have a short stay. The flat did not measure up to the European standards of living. Looking very shabby, not much was left of its life. The handle of the tiny bathroom window had fallen off. The floor of the sitting-room creaked woefully. All the furniture was either broken or had cracks in it. Yet sometimes, one must be content with the least possible things in life, which was what I had to do. I was, therefore, prepared to accept it and live in my new home without the slightest shilly-shallying.

I felt good that I had found a home I could not share with anyone, and my son could sit and watch children's programmes. I also felt good knowing that no eyes would watch over me; I could chuck my clothes anywhere I liked and sing while I was taking a shower.

And what is more, one can live in a furnished house, on the furniture of which one has no claims, to focus on one's daily affairs. Moreover, I had to live in the district where the mother and the father of the child I was carrying in my belly lived so they would know how I was getting on. Here Afshaar played the role of a middleman. The couple had credited the second instalment they owed me into Afshaar's account and were supposed to pay me the final instalment after the child was born. As I could not open a bank account, all my money was kept in Afshaar's account. He agreed that he would pay one-hundred-thousand Kroner to Hooshyaar when he attended the interview at the Immigration Office. All of this wheeling and dealing had to be done illegally.

A few days after I started working in Afshaar's restaurant, I made the acquaintance of Goli. She was an Iranian girl who made a living by working in restaurants and hotels in Stockholm. She studied computer science at the University of Stockholm, even though she had a degree from an Iranian university. Our friendship began when Goli came to work in Afshaar's restaurant. After discovering my problems, she found somewhere decent for me to live. She was a twenty-nine-old, slim brunette. She often wore bizarre dresses, such as a red, laddered tight and short, split skirt. With black hair and large eyes, she had a hot personality and a sense of humour. She had come to Sweden on her own and wanted to stay on. As her student visa was about to expire, she was looking for a steady job to extend her stay. She had rented student accommodation in the Solna

Municipality. She would talk about her room as if it was the size of a grave that had no room to swing a cat in! She soon left Afshaar's restaurant.

'Stay away from Iranians here,' she would tell me. 'They're all charlatans! You're not a donkey to work for thirty Kroner an hour.'

She insisted that we should both go and live in the city. I explained to her that, in my situation, I was unable to do anything or go anywhere. All that I was doing seemed foolish to her – such as renting my womb and being in that sham marriage. Nothing made sense, in her opinion. In truth, staying in this country was ultimate foolishness! Every day she would repeat many times she wanted to return to Iran!

Having been in Sweden for four years when I met her, she knew all the ins and outs of living here and could be of great help. I found her so sympathetic that I trusted her instinctively. She told me she had seen everything strange in her first days in Sweden and kept looking open-mouthed at things and people. I, too, told her about my frustrations at obtaining residency here and finding a place to stay. I never understood why she tried so hard to find a job and stay here. She reminded me of the character of Eagle in the Gulliver's Travels cartoon, who always kept saying: 'I know, I know.'

I admired her courage and her gift of repartee. With her self-confidence (which was lacking me), she could communicate intimately with people. One morning she invited me to the Grand Hotel, where she served breakfast from five until ten. She would then leave to attend her lectures. She would work for an hour in a restaurant or a fast-food shop in the afternoons. Some evenings in the holidays and weekends, she would work in the locker-rooms of bars and discos. Being an unusual character, she fascinated me. That's why she became my best friend. After that, we saw one another less and less. She didn't have time to come and see me thanks to her work and studies. Finally, one day she phoned me out of the blue and told me to run out of the restaurant to where she was waiting. However hard I insisted on the phone that she must come into the restaurant she said she was in a rush and asked me to go out!

An icy wind was blowing outside, and the sky was overcast. 'Take a look at the sky!' she said thoughtfully.

'So?' I said.

'Listen. Don't expect to see wonders here,' she said with a lump in her throat. 'There's another, much harsher side to life here. At least in our own country, we were somebody for ourselves. But we're nothing but second-class citizens here! Do you get it? We're nothing but black-haired foreigners.'

I listened without saying anything.

'I hope I didn't upset you,' she went on. 'I feel very down. I'm tired of this life of vagabondage here!'

'I think I understand what you're saying,' I said. 'Truth be told, I'm in the same boat as you.'

'Anyway, I've got good news for you,' she said suddenly. 'I've found a home for you. Didn't I tell you I keep my word? I've found a cottage for you. The bugger is that it'll take about one-and-a-half hours to get there from Stockholm. The good thing about it is that you can stay there as long as you like until your situation is sorted. The house belongs to the uncle of one of my friends. The cottage is close to a large villa where an old couple live. I've told them about you and the pickle you're in, and they've agreed to let you stay there.' She hugged me before leaving and added: 'There's no hurry! You've still got plenty of time! We're now midwinter, and they can't find a tenant easily. So just let me know how you're getting on!'

Later on, I told Afshaar all about the cottage.

'No, this is not going to work,' he said. 'It's not a good idea for a single, pregnant woman with a child to live in a remote village! Wait a little while, please.' He then pointed to my bulging belly and said: 'You must now focus on the baby in your belly. You must first sort out this task. God will take care of everything after that.'

Hooshyaar was supposed to go to the Immigration Office to fill out the forms of our marriage and give them the cottage address so that I could register Danial's name in the nearby nursery.

'Leave everything to me,' he used to say. 'I'll take care of it.'

I was filled with fear, mistrust, and suspicion about him from the word go. It seemed to me he was hiding his roguishness behind a façade of goodwill. There was something fake about his kindness that made me not believe him. It was as if he had taken it upon himself to play the role of a saviour. He made me feel neither hopeless nor hopeful! He showed a sort of affectionate compassion towards Danial and kept repeating that it was not suitable for a single woman and a child...! He kept talking about the Norrtälje Prison where they took the asylum-seekers. Sometimes you are injected with something to keep you calm throughout the journey. Other times you are taken first to the Immigration Office in Märsta near Stockholm Arlanda Airport and put into a chartered plane to be sent back to Iran.

When I told Goli all about this she lost her temper.

'Tell him to go to hell!' she shouted. 'They are all liars. They're all in this together.'

Maybe she was right, for Afshaar himself had introduced Hooshyaar to me. When I asked him later on about him he said to me: 'Suit yourself. I don't know much about him. I only know that he has got seven kids.' But Hooshyaar had a different story about his kids.

'No. I've got six kids, one of whom is my brother's whom I've brought here from Iraq to get child benefit for him.'

Hooshyaar was an extremely ugly man without a single redeeming feature to help one turn a blind eye to his ugliness. His nose was so flat that it covered half of his face. He had a dark complexion and his arms and chest were covered in frizzy black hair.

'Who's the father of this baby in your belly?' he asked me one day when he was in a kind mood. 'Why doesn't he do anything for you? He has no doubt left you! What's the world coming to! Well, it takes all sorts to make a world!'

No sooner had I settled in the cottage than I began to use detergent to obsessively clean all the bathroom walls, the kitchen walls, the fridge, and the cooker. All this took longer than I thought. However hard I washed, everything was still filthy. That's why I couldn't bring myself to feel at home in the cottage. The roof was invaded with ravens. With the faintest sound they would flap their wings. Sometimes they would fix their beady little eyes into the cottage. Seeing them would churn my stomach. I found their gaze very scary. You would have thought they were auguring bad news. I was overcome with an ominous feeling.

Very soon, I started to buy the things I needed for the cottage. I went to the Jula Store in the Arninge Shopping Centre and bought a blanket, two pillows, a towel, a pan, plates, mugs, and some cutlery. Meanwhile, I began to cook nutritious Iranian foods. Every day I would visit a nearby shop and buy fresh ingredients. However, I had no appetite at all.

Christmas was nearly there. Looking at the people around me, I envied their everyday lives, preparing for the festive season with enthusiasm, all of them doing the same things; giving presents to each other, sitting around the Christmas tree, listening to Christmas songs, eating the same food in all the houses, and listening to similar Christmas prayers in most of the countries. All in all, this added to my feelings of isolation and loneliness.

After I put things in order somewhat in my new home, I took Danial to the city where Goli joined us, and we looked at the Christmas lights in the streets and shops. One day before noon, Hooshyaar climbed the stairs and knocked on the door. Danial opened the door without looking at me. Hooshyaar was standing outside the door holding a plastic Christmas tree. He walked in without asking, placed the tree near the telly, sat himself on the sofa, and started talking to Danial. Not knowing what to say, I waited for him to go away. I went to the kitchen and busied myself for long enough until he left.

I kept saying to myself this man was trying to help us.

'Do you realise that if they arrest you now, you'll be deported right away!' he kept warning me, posing as a benevolent man. 'That's why I'm trying to help you. I'll sort out your residency. Look. You don't mess around here with the law!'

He had begun to talk about my appearance – for example, how pretty I was and so on. It wasn't easy to hear such a hideous-looking man admiring me.

'Before going to the Immigration Office, we must agree on what we're going to tell them about one another,' he said one day. 'It's highly likely that right at the first interview, they might ask you what the colour of my underpants ....'

Hearing this, I felt sick and asked him politely but firmly to stop. Seeing how upset I was, he changed his tune immediately and said: 'No. They might ask you what the colour of my toothbrush is, or what colour the duvet under which we....' I didn't let him finish his sentence.

'These are the things they'll be asking on later occasions,' I said after a pause. 'For the moment, you should only have to declare that....'

'No. It's not going to be as easy as that,' he said with a broad smile that revealed his crowned teeth. 'Once I've sorted out the house for you, the rest will be all right!'

He breathed out the foul smell in his mouth. The back of his head was flat, as if someone had whacked him hard there. This made him look like one of those retarded men. I was supposed to pay him the first instalment of one-hundred-thousand Kroner and the rest I owed him once his job was done. Needing him to help me to realise my hopes, I had to put up with him.

Sometimes hearing his footfalls on the steps, I would pretend I was not at home. I would immediately put the lights out, turn off the telly, hand the iPad to Danial, and remain dead silent, not even flushing the toilet so I could get rid of him.

Things were bad enough in my life. Facing dilemmas such as this, one has to accept the lesser of two evils. I, too, had to obtain, as soon as possible, my leave to remain document. If Hooshyaar signed my papers,, they would more quickly grant me my leave to remain. I could then go to the American Embassy as quickly as possible, show them my invitation letter that my uncle signed on behalf of the Jewish Iranian Society, and apply for a visa. I was determined never to return to Iran. I also made up my mind that once I left Sweden, I would never return to this cold part of the world where I knew no one, had no motivation or had nothing to write home about. I knew I would be safe on the other side of the planet. My grandfather was the first member of his family who had gone to America. Because of his efforts, the rest of his family ended up in the best part of America. A few years before the Revolution, my dad helped my uncle to emigrate to America. Although my uncle was a doctor in Iran, they wouldn't let him practice his profession in America. During his first years there, my grandfather helped my uncle become qualified again. Once he obtained his practice permit, he set up a surgery in New Jersey. Soon after, my other uncle joined him, followed by my aunt and her children. To cut a long story short, they were living in California. My father was the only brother who could not leave Iran after the Revolution because he was in the army. His being also a Jew didn't help the matter at all. Besides, my father wanted to reap the benefits of all his years of hard work. He knew very well that if he left Iran, he would never be able to return. This would mean losing his pension – the fruits of his years of hard work in the Iranian Navy. My father was a patriot. He had the conviction that no matter what religion or faith we believe in, we are indebted to the land in which we are born.

'When my time comes, I'd like to die here,' he used to say. 'I'd like to be buried beside my ancestors. Here's where they took gave their last gasp. Here's where they've shed tears of joy and sadness. All my existence is part of this soil. This is my home.'

His words kept echoing in my mind. Iran was his home.

He had always looked after his wife, sisters and brothers and being indebted to my father; they wanted to help me at all costs. All my cousins, men and women alike, were now living in New York and California, like a large tribe or clan. This made me even sadder. I felt I was far away from everyone. I kept imagining that something was the cause of my isolation, making me feel that I was somebody special.

Just before ten o'clock at night, I heard the doorbell ring.

'Oh, the usual pest!' I said to myself. 'I'll not open the door.'

He knocked again. Lowering my voice, I stuck my head out of the half-open door, not letting him come in. I stood behind the door. He was standing outside, holding a box of chocolate in his hand.

'Has anything happened that you've come this time of night?' I asked.

'I've come to see Danial,' he answered nonchalantly as if he was chewing gum.

'He went to sleep a long time ago,' I said quietly.

He put out his ungainly hands, offering the box of chocolates to me.

'No, thanks,' I said coldly.

Insisting that I should accept it, he said: 'What size is Danial? I want to buy him a Christmas present. My cousin has a clothes boutique in Kista, and I can get whatever you want.'

'No, thanks,' I said. 'Danial has enough clothes.'

But he was far more pig-headed than I thought. He stood there, hopping from one foot to another. I took the box of chocolate from his hands and shut the door in his face without saying a word. I waited until I heard his footfalls receding down the stairs.

I locked the door from behind and said to myself: 'I must not let him in! I must not open the door when he comes here, and I must never talk to him again! I must look after myself and Danial. I mustn't let him climb those stairs again.' I returned to the bedroom, pulled the duvet over Danial, and listened to his breathing. I stood beside the bed and looked at him. I'd been doing this ritual of standing beside his bed and listening to the rhythm of his breathing. The light in the room had fallen on Danial's face, he looked as innocent as that of an angel or a saint. It was as if the sound of his breathing calmed me down.

I loved this sense of oneness with him – living in the knowledge that a being needs me in this world, knowing that I am a haven for someone, and being aware of the truth that this small body was part of my existence. I gently touched his earlobe and kissed the mole behind his ear.

I began to murmur a piece of a poem that my brother used to recite. You would have thought this poem was a magical magic, a spiritual communion between my brother and me. I sang the piece to myself:

Life is like water,
If it does not flow, it will be isolated.
The bud of a smile will perish in the sad waters of a still
pond.
Love, like gazelles, will not drink from its muddied
waters,
The birds of ecstasy will not come into being from the
depths of its mirror.

I picked up my mobile, went into the kitchen, and sent a text to Goli. In a short text, she told me she would work till four o'clock in the morning. I sat down on a chair beside the table. I was desperate for a glass of wine but couldn't drink as I was carrying a baby in my belly. I filled up the kettle, placed it on the cooker, and turned on the radio broadcasting Beethoven's Fifth Symphony – a succession of sounds that were serenely receding into the distance.

I listened to the hissings of the gas-flames and the regular gurgling of the water in the kettle. I got up and stood there. Silence reigned in the street. I could not hear a single noise outside from time to time; a car passed by in the far distance. Snow was falling, and everywhere was white. I was scared to look out of the window. Using my fingers, I counted the months before the baby's delivery.

***

It was New Year's Eve, and being a red-letter day, everybody had retreated to their homes. I stayed at home the whole day. Heavy snow was falling. I glanced at the bus timetable. I thought I would take Danial to the city so that he could watch the fireworks. We got on the bus and got off in front of the Max fast-food restaurant in Näsbypark. The restaurant was deserted except for me, my son, and a few young men and women working in the kitchen. I only ordered a child's meal. I had no appetite. My stomach was upset with heartburn. I had heard that pregnant women become sick like this when the hair grows on the baby's head. I had no feelings towards this baby. When I was pregnant with Danial, I meditated and listened to Bach and Beethoven. Every week I ate frankincense so that he would become an intelligent child. I sang for him for hours whenever I was having a bath. I didn't even want to feel this baby in my belly. It wriggled so much in my stomach that it made me very agitated.

The youth who worked behind the counter brought us a tray with a child's meal. He had a white hat on, and a red, florescent Christmas star was stuck to his shirt. He brought us a plastic penny whistle and a few red balloons. Another followed him with a tray on which were two cheeseburgers. Both of them wished me a 'Happy New Year'.

I felt as if they had insulted me. Surprised, I said to them: 'I only ordered one cheeseburger.' At that moment, the sky was lit with shooting blue and silver fountains that turned into flowers or stars. This was followed by louder and louder explosions, after which the sky turned red again. The spectrum of coloured lights formed in the sky looked like palm trees that opened up for an instant and vanished. My grandmother used to say that a palm tree is a strange tree. It is similar to a human being; no matter how deep its roots are in the soil, if you prune the fronds on its crown, it will soon wither and die (that's why the units used to count them are 'persons' just like human beings). They had chopped off our heads as they do palm trees. Our heads having been chopped off, we had become deracinated human beings, both in our country and here.

Feeling lonely, I felt humiliated. I longed for our Persian New Year. I was sitting here all by myself; there were neither colourful foods nor presents. There was nothing for me here but a long, boring holiday. There was only cold and loneliness here. The more I pondered, the more I realised I was happy in those days in my homeland. When our past recedes into the mist of time, we mostly recall the happy memories that make us feel calm and at peace.

Why was this happing? Why should one change one's country? I was under the illusion that if I changed my homeland, I would change myself. But I was the same person as before, dragging my former self with me.

I only ate a few chips with ketchup without touching that cursed hamburger. When we decided to return home, we missed the bus. Being a holiday meant there would be no buses for hours from Röda dagar. I felt more and more like a homeless tramp as I stood with a child at the bus stop on a night like this.

I was not in the mood to get on a bus or train. On these cold, wintry days, the thought of being in a metro or a bus made me sick. I wouldn't say I liked the civilised-looking, well-dressed men in suits wearing leather-gloves who averted their eyes from you, the women in formal, funereal-looking dresses who stood on the descending escalator, the tall, large man who spat his spit at your feet, the rude youth who banged my face with his rucksack. This girl sat beside me and gazed at YouTube at the programme that showed how best to use eyeshadow while munching a juicy apple that drove me mad. This youth stuck his head to his mobile and listened to an awful singer that droned in my ear. But that night, Danial and I were the only passengers on the bus. After arriving home, I felt we had been on an hour-long journey.

There was no news of Hooshyaar until a week after Christmas. Everywhere was still closed. The whole city was strangely silent. The sparkle of the neon lights in the street was pouring into the sitting-room through the kitchen window. I was stretching on the sofa near the telly, listening to the wriggling of the tadpole in my belly that had disturbed my sleep. I was unable to sleep on my side. As I lay there on my back, I was trying to watch a movie on the telly. Sometimes, when you watch something on the telly to distract yourself, it is as if you forget all about the time and place you're in. That's what my father has done lately. With the glare of the light from the telly reflecting on his glasses, he would sit motionless in front of it. You could never figure out what he was thinking about.

Around midnight, I heard the house's front door open. I turned my head and looked at the door from the window that overlooked the entrance door. I saw him standing at the door of the sitting room no sooner than my heart missed a beat. First, I closed my eyes and made it seem as if I was asleep. I wished I would never open my eyes and see those black, blood-shot, puffy eyes staring at me. Next, he stroked my arm, which made me recoil in horror. He gripped my arm firmly with one hand, pressed his face against mine, and opened his fly with the other. When I tried to scream with all my might, he let go of my arm, pressed his hand on my mouth, and thrust all his weight on to me with extraordinary strength. My back against the sofa, I was unable to move.

His wet armpits smelt of the sweat of a sexually excited that I had never smelt before. His heart was pounding hard. The enlarged pupils of his bulging eyes, like those of a cow, were fixed on mine. He kept saying: 'I'll get your residency.' I kept scratching his face and digging my manicured nails into his cheeks and body. Suddenly he withdrew himself and punched me so hard in the face that I tumbled to the floor. He threw himself on me like a vicious brute as I lay there. He pulled down my knickers. As I struggled on the floor, I stretched my hand and grabbed something from the top of the small table in front of the sofa. I didn't know what the object was – a plate, a bowl, a jug. Whatever it was, I hit his head and face with it till the top of his head was gashed, and blood began to trickle down his face. My blows, not being effective, not only didn't work but enraged and strengthened him. He blocked my mouth tightly with his hand. Finally, having resigned myself to the worst, I gave up the struggle. Seeing that he had a hard-on, I knew that no power could slacken his penis. I thought I was finished. Soaking with sweat, he kept repeating in an inhuman voice: 'I'll get the residency, the residency!' I tried hard to stop his penis from penetrating me. He was now moaning and groaning: 'All the orifices of a pregnant woman are tight!'

I thought, what would happen to Danial if I died! I didn't mind what he would do to me as long as he wouldn't kill me. I had to be there for Danial, whom I loved. All that was left for me in this world was my son. I closed my eyes until he finished the job. No more sounds came out of his dark lips.

It all happened very quickly. All that had taken no more than a few minutes, during which Danial was asleep. It was a miracle that he didn't wake up. Then, without hanging around, Hooshyaar, while belting up his trousers, said: 'If you breathe a word to anyone, I'll report you to the police, and they'll throw you into Norrtälje Prison,' He added, pointing his finger to the sky: '*Hejdå*'. He then let out a short laugh that sounded like the whinnying of a horse.

I felt such a sharp pain on the right side of my belly that I couldn't breathe. The baby was still in the right place but wasn't moving. All I could think of was that I was alive. My only worry was that Danial might be scared. Standing up, I noticed a liquid trickling down between my legs. Thinking at first that it was blood, I touched it. The stinking gooey liquid was, in fact, his semen. I thought of going to the police station, but I was afraid. I could raise their suspicions. They would then ask to see my identity documents, asking me uncomfortable questions and wanting to see my leave to remain papers.

The border checks had been going on for a long time. I was unable to go anywhere by train. I had no choice but to wait. Any minute the inspectors could get on the train and ask for documents. I could no longer stay in the cottage, not even a second. I had to leave; I had to.... The best thing I could do was to contact Goli.

5

I had read this somewhere by Becket, who said: 'You must go on. I can't go on. I'll go on. Try again. Fail again. Fail better!'

I got on the bus and sat down. I kept gazing at the windscreen-wipers, the swirling snowflakes that melted when they settled on the windows. Danial's head, resting on my lap, was soaked in sweat even though it was cold. I stroked his head, feeling sorry for him as I knew what a wretched farcical life was ahead of him.

A few snowploughs were driving in the opposite direction on the other side of the motorway. Their rotating flashing lights looked like blood-shot eyes that gleamed from the other side of the motorway. All those moving lights in that gloomy silence appeared to bode ill. All throughout the journey I kept swearing at the parents of the baby that was in my belly, cursing my luck. I imagined some ominous plots were being hatched for me behind my back. I thought of the money

I'd given to Afshaar, the three-month deposit I'd given
to Hoshyaar. All that money had, no doubt, gone. I had
to do something. If I had a gun I would have definitely
gone back and killed both of them. I was able to make
out Hoshyaar's breath from miles away in order to kill
him. I was pretty sure I could empty all the bullets in
him!

Danial moved his head that he had rested on my
bulging belly. An older man beside me reading a
newspaper lifted his head and glanced at Danial.
Carrying a child on my lap and another in my belly, I
knew I looked pale!

The bus turned into a by-road, and the snow fell more
heavily. A village covered with snow soon emerged. The
road that passed through a jungle became more and
more winding as the bus moved on. Arriving finally at a
church on the edge of the village, we stopped one stop
before the bus station. With his head dangling like the
head of a lifeless rabbit, Danial weighed as light as straw.
My heavy bag was pulling on my shoulder.

It was dark even though it was just past noon. I didn't
have the faintest idea as to what to do next. I couldn't
even pronounce the name of that village. The tall maple
trees had added to the darkness, making it appear even
thicker. I could hear the throbbing of the blood in my
temples.

I began to look for the address Goli had given me. Unfortunately, everything in this village seemed either black or white. No, everything was shrouded in black and white, shades of grey, rather like the gloomy mood you find in those Eastern European films that deepen the feeling of melancholy and desolation in you.

Further up the bus station appeared a yellow building, looking like a proud ship that had run aground. It was a two-storey manor house with a rusty, sloping roof and a slanting porch. You would have thought the dried-up ivies that had covered all the walls around the house were holding up the whole edifice, stopping it from falling apart. Opposite the building was a vast garden that extended to a distance devoid of any views. Several weather-beaten rocks stood here and there in the grounds at the far ends of which a few villas whose inhabitants had apparently left months ago could be seen. I stood outside the main gate. I thought that was the address as it was the only house with lights on. I rang the bell that wasn't working. I pushed the gate that opened with a creaking sound and stepped into the yard. There was no bell near the entrance of the large building. I knocked on the door with my frozen knuckles. No one answered. Danial was frozen, and I had become numb with cold. The baby in my belly had curled itself into a ball. I knocked on the door again—

still no sound from inside. I climbed the porch steps and went round the building where I had seen the light. I trod in a pool of water. Hearing someone open the door, I turned and climbed the steps. A tall older man was standing at the doorway. I introduced myself. He neither greeted me nor welcomed me. After glancing at Danial, he disappeared inside the house and returned, holding several keys. He stepped out and began to walk, followed by Danial and me. He looked seventy or maybe more. The wrinkles on his face reminded me of the winding road in the jungle. From a distance, the cottage seemed much humbler than the main building. It was a small country house that looked like it had been built in a hurry. The older man opened the cottage door and welcomed us as a landlord would. Inside the cottage, it wasn't as cold and unpleasant as outside. The heat inside the room warmed our faces. We quickly took off our shoes and stepped inside. The cottage had two large rooms and a kitchen. In the kitchen was a table with Christmas things on it. The air inside was charming. On top of the table were lots of mince pies, usually eaten during Christmas. There were Christmas decorations with tiny lights behind all the windows.

The cottage smelt of fresh air. We walked along a long corridor that led to a drawing-room. Paintings with bright colours hung from the walls, and shelves were full of books. All this seemed like a sweet dream; I imagined myself being like a little girl in a fairy-tale who sold match-boxes while dreaming of her grandmother's house. Danial kept rubbing his eyes with the back of his hand. After pointing out the coffee-maker to me, the man put it on. The aroma of the coffee floated in the air. Then, as if he wanted to show me everything was in working order, he switched on the radio. He went into the sitting room and turned on the telly. A woman was standing beside a map, forecasting heavy snow and possible road-closures, warning the citizens to take the necessary precautions. I looked at the older man's face and smiled. He smiled back at me and handed over the keys to me calmly and formally; he tried to speak slowly and clearly. He then stroked Danial's head and left.

When coming here on the bus, I saw an Ica minimarket just before the bus station. Danial had to go to the toilet. I took off his clothes, found a cup in the cabinet, and made coffee myself. I washed Danial's face and hands. Seeing all this difficult to believe, I became very excited. I put on Danial's winter coat, and we both went to the Ica minimarket. Although it was a small food market, it had what we needed. We bought quite a lot of foodstuff and quickly returned home. I switched on the telly for Danial, and I sprawled on the sofa. I touched my belly. The baby stirred a bit.

I had a fever due to exhaustion. I got up, walked to the window, and stuck my feverish face to the glass covered with a thin sheet of ice from outside. I inserted the new SIM card I had bought from the store into my mobile, phoned Goli, and told her my unique number. I let her know that everything was all right. She promised she would call on us as soon as possible and said that she hadn't forgotten about Danial's Christmas present.

'We're all somewhat outsiders here,' she said. 'I don't want anything bad happening to you. It was a good thing that you left Stockholm. The village is better for you. I told the older man all about your predicaments. They seem quite nice and are very sorry for the horrible things that have happened to you.'

The nights seemed so long here that you wondered if morning would ever come. I chucked my pillow to one side, hugged Danial tightly, and closed my eyes.

When I woke up, the sun was high in the sky. It took me a long time to move my arms and legs. I was stretching like a mummy on that damp sheet. Having slept deeply as though I had been in a coma, I felt I had had enough rest, but I still wanted to go on sleeping even more. I thought of freshening myself up with a nice hot shower. Danial was playing with his iPad in the sitting-room. I stood before a tall mirror with a carved wooden frame to wrap the towel round my wet, untidy hair. I regarded myself in the mirror. I felt sick looking at the layers of fat on my thighs. It was as if I was blown up like a balloon. My face had gone as round as a plate, my eyes were puffy, and my breasts were swollen. Another life, whose sudden movements scared me, was stirring in my belly. I no longer had a small nose and a slim body that made me look like a young girl. Neither was I that young girl who needed moral support. When I pushed aside the last lock of my hair, I thought of Sina.

I had forgotten many things in my life; for example, my twentieth birthday or wedding anniversary and other important landmarks. But I can never forget my brother's face. He was ten years older than me. He was in high school when I was in Year One of primary school. Bing was knowledgeable; he was very good at all subjects. He studied and read books all the time. All he did was study. He was a mathematics genius and had won many prizes in mathematics competitions. For him, life was nothing but numbers. We were exact opposites. As I grew up, my parents noticed more and more the differences between my brother and me.

I had never been a good daughter to them, but my brother was a good son. I don't know what was so wrong with me that they had never brought themselves to like me. Maybe it was because they had never wanted a second child. I had heard my mother say several times that my father had stopped talking to her for days because she had not taken measures not to become pregnant. I had also heard her say that she had tried all sorts of tricks, such as taking pills or jumping up and down the steps, to get rid of me. None of those ploys had worked. I was five-years-old when I heard my mother talking about me to her colleagues 'Even when she was in my belly, she was obstinate and difficult.'

My relationship with Sina was of a different kind. I was always my brother's sweet little sister. Sometimes roles get swapped in a family. It was as if he had become my father by helping me with my homework and listening to my childish ramblings that, sometimes, made him laugh out loud. Whenever I came home from school he would sit beside me, imploring me to tell him about my day without leaving anything out. Nothing would ever escape his keen attention. You would have thought he was my protector. Every morning he would accompany me to my school. He would even upset my parents for letting me return home alone. He was the best brother a sister could wish for.

Whenever I was with him in the lane or the streets, I felt safe under his watchful eyes. Being beside him made me think that people would take notice of me, making me feel good about myself. He perhaps was trying to understand me because I was fragile and sensitive.

Nevertheless, he never stopped me from doing what I wanted, letting me do whatever I liked.

I can't say precisely when and how people come of age. I know, however, that my brother was a grown-up in those days. I used to muse over the fact that I would never grow up like him. Likewise, Sina has always remained a grown-up in my mind. He was no more than twelve when he won the medal for the best swimmer in the Tehran school competitions. His room was full of awards.

My mathematical ability was scandalous, and I never learned to swim, crawl, or butterfly. Most of the time, I didn't do my homework after school. That's why my father was always angry with me, looking for excuses to punish me.

My brother, however, would say to my parents: 'No. What she needs most are care and encouragement.' He showered me with so much praise and commendation that it made me feel euphoric for hours. He would always tell me: 'You're unique only because it's you!' Despite our age gap, we had an extraordinary relationship. He was wonderfully full of life. After school, I would rush to his room, where he was studying. I would lie on the floor beside him. An American flag hung on the wall beside his bed. I remember him pointing at the flag, saying: 'Do you see how those stars twinkle with happiness? This is the flag of the promised land.' He believed that Jewish people should live in their land. However, he always said, 'We don't belong here.'

Without any warning, he suddenly left. He had gone to his promised land, and he never came back. As a result, my period began earlier than the normal time. One day when I went out of the toilet, my grandmother, who was staying with us, slapped me hard on the cheek, leaving me baffled. She followed me to my room and said: 'I slapped you so that your cheeks will always remain as red as pomegranate flowers. Sticking to an ancient tradition, a girl, who has her first period, must be slapped so that her cheeks will become as red as pomegranate flowers.' I grabbed her hand and asked: 'Please, nana, promise me you won't tell my mum about my period?' She gave me her word.

Having done all the preparations for Sina's trip to America, my father thought it would be best for Sina to leave Iran before they called him for mandatory military service.

My father had asked everyone not to tell me about Sina's forthcoming departure as that year; I was going to sit my final year nation-wide exams. I was told that Sina had gone to one of the provinces to revise for the nation-wide university entrance exams. After he was gone, I never again talked to my brother over the phone, refusing even to answer his letters at the back, which twinkled the stars of happiness. My father would tell me: 'Go on, drop a line to your brother, you obstinate girl!' My mother would say, 'Is this how you repay him for being so kind to you?'

Sina didn't take long to reach the status of an outstanding model among all the relatives. He had always been treated somewhat as a divinity by them. He was no longer a boy. In the photos he sent us from America, he looked like a man, something I could not come to terms with. Not so much as uttering a word to me, he had left. Every day when I returned home from school, I would go to his room and lie on his bed.

In his room, I would look at the objects and medals he had won in his swimming competitions. If he were in Iran, he would have been sleeping here. Instead, he would draw the duvet up to his chest, clasp his hands and fold his legs. Now all that was left of him in the room was his scent.

I felt I had returned to those years when I enjoyed banal and curious things—for example, a pen in the form of a naked woman or his snakes-and-ladders game. Under the mantelpiece near the window, there was a place where he kept his books. The mantelpiece, on top of which were heaped many books, was made of wood from the oak tree in our yard. The books were so heavy that the oak tree could hold them. He jealously guarded *Moby Dick* by Herman Melville and Hemmingway's *The Old Man and the Sea*. When I picked up the books, I saw a brown shoebox concealed behind them. Taking the lid off the box, I saw colourful marbles of different sizes, a few of my butterfly-shaped hairclips, and a diary in which he had scribbled in his handwriting. I knew his writing so well as he wrote my homework for me occasionally. At the bottom of the shoebox, I unearthed a number of love letters that my brother did not write. The scribbles were illegible. However carefully I looked at the notes, I couldn't find the name of the person who wrote them. I found that strange. I never knew anything about my brother's affairs of the heart. I took the love-letters and put the shoebox back in its place. I read the letters over and over. On each letter was stuck a red-lipsticked mouth print. I read the letters so many times that the lipstick faded.

One day when I returned home from school, I noticed that my mother had taken away the objects from Sina's room, changing it into a sitting-room by placing a telly and a three-seater sofa in it. No sign of the former room was left. Even the America flag with its pale stars had gone. My mother said, 'The flag had gone threadbare, and I threw it away!' She was right. Everything will be in tatters one day, even the memories of the people we love.

When I realised that my brother had gone to America for good, I began sleepless nights. Even my parents couldn't understand why I had become an insomniac. Sometimes I remained awake till morning, staring at the ceiling. I remember every night I was given a herbal infusion, hot milk or a bowl of yoghurt mixed with sour orange blossoms, and I was forced to drink up all of them. Finally, I was taken to the best doctors in town to be examined. Unfortunately, none of the doctors could help me, and I was as sleepless as ever.

This sorry state of affairs carried on for a long time. I felt unwell and listless all the time. Every evening I would either sit in the kitchen or go to my bedroom and roam around the house throughout the night.

'You mustn't stay awake all night,' my father said. 'It's bad for a child of your age.'

I became an insomniac again. Frightened and anxious, I would fall into a fitful sleep every night, constantly waking with a start, imagining that Hoshyaar was standing outside the window. The slightest noise would startle me out of my slumber. I was afraid of Hoshyaar and my future. I desperately needed human contact, so I longed for someone to hug me. I felt cold. I wanted someone to look after me, someone strong who would hold me tight, a force to stop me in this time and place from tumbling into the abyss.

There were no other houses at the back of this cottage. One could only see agricultural lands and woods through which a dark road stretched up to the horizon. I was so scared that at night I kept waking up with a start. I felt so cold that it was as if my body had been frozen. Feeling unsafe, I felt as if fear had penetrated my blood. After nightfall, I could hear the barking of dogs, or maybe they were the hyenas laughing. Whatever they were, they sounded freakish to me. Most of the time, the shrieking of a woman could be heard from among the trees. Darkness reigned outside the window, and I kept all the lights on until morning. This, however, didn't help as the house was surrounded from all sides by an impenetrable, invisible wall of darkness!

The nights were growing longer and longer, and the slow shortening of the days made me feel increasingly lonely and condemned, fearing the lengthening of the time in the dark. I could hear the muffled howling of the wind that rattled the windows and the sound of the branches that snapped under the weight of heavy snow.

Feeling desolate and abandoned, I thought I was cut off from everything and everyone. The hatred I nursed for Hoshyaar had deepened. The blow that I had suffered was so brutal that it made me ill all the time and knocked me down so hard that I had no strength left in me to rise to my feet.

***

Don't tell the tale of 'Snow White' to your baby crows,
They cannot cope with the nightmare of being
discriminated against!

Life in this ugly place seemed hopeless and wearying. I kept telling myself how alien their world was to me. This remote and soulless village was like an endless labyrinth that would have hidden unexpected troubles for me for a long time.

I would sit for hours beside Danial, asking him to draw pictures for me, images that were no more than some lines that didn't make much sense. 'What have you drawn for Mummy?' I would ask him.

'This is you, Mummy,' he would say.

'But this drawing has no hands or legs,' I would say. 'Where's the head?'

'These are her eyes, these are her legs, and this is her head,' he would show me after a pause.

I didn't know what to do or for how long I would have to stay here with this child. I was far too helpless to make a decision. All I could do, at least, was resign myself to the passage of time until I delivered this cargo I carried in my belly.

The only coffee shop in the village was also a post office selling tickets, which was opposite the church. The owner was a bulky middle-aged man who always sat behind the till. When a customer entered the shop, he was not in the mood to stand up or say hello. He had arranged the items about him on the shelves so that he could reach them easily. He would only need to put out his arm to get hold of the lotto tickets and the scratch cards. He did the postal services himself and sold cigarettes, coffee, and Smorgas Torta sandwiches. His was the only shop where you could buy hot food. No sooner would Danial go near the candies or candies than the man would crane forward, giving me a black look.

As Danial needed fresh air, I took him to the park beside the church. He could hardly walk in his full-length anorak. We arrived at a spot where some children made snowmen with their templates. Danial just stood there, clutching his spade and not daring to step forward. A woman was sitting on a nearby bench with her face glued to her mobile phone without paying attention to the children. When Danial wanted to step onto the patch of snow, the woman raised her head and shot a sharp glance at him. Looking at her, I knew she was only thinking about one thing: 'These people must be foreigners.' Danial had barely put one foot inside the play area when the little boy shouted at him: 'You're not allowed to come in here!'

Hearing this, Danial stood there gazing at the boy! His mother, wearing an anorak that looked like the ones worn by Eskimos and a fur hat, got up and began to talk rapidly to Danial. I gathered from the tone of her voice that she was telling Danial he shouldn't play there and must go and play somewhere else! Knowing that I would make a laughing-stock of myself by intervening, I felt I couldn't join in. I got to my feet, standing there without taking a step. I looked dishevelled and scruffy. The zip of my knitwear cardigan I was wearing was stuck half-way up. I didn't feel confident enough to talk to the woman. All of my clothes had become too small for me. Unable to buckle the belt of my jeans, I had left the top button undone, instead using an elastic band that I had attached with a safety pin to the belt from inside.

'Why don't you go to the H&M Store and buy a good deal of cheap clothes to wear during your pregnancy?' Goli had said to me time and time again. 'Sales are on now. Go on and do a spot of shopping. Otherwise, you'll come down with some illness. What would you do if you caught a chill on your sides?'

I was afraid of moving if my trousers fell in front of the woman. She tried to stop Danial from going into the play area. Her small daughter had now joined in, screaming as if she had seen a scary creature. For an instant, I thought of getting up and pulling the woman's ponytail that was stuck out from the back of her fur hat, but I wouldn't dare take part in that quarrel.

Ignoring the little boy's mother, Danial walked into the play area, which caused the boy to holler, filling the air. He chucked a handful of snow at Danial, who, to get his own back, delivered a kick with unheard-of strength to the boy's snowman that crumbled into a heap with its nose – a carrot that is – sprawling on the ground. Seeing this, I plucked up courage, ran to Danial, who had put his hands on his ears and was howling non-stop, and lifted him. I saw at the same time how the little boy's mother grabbed her son's arm, threw a hard look at Danial and said in a loud voice: 'Bloody foreigners!'

After days of uninterrupted snowfall, the sun finally came out one day, shining on the snow everywhere. After long, grey and dismal days of being stuck at home, I longed to see the sun. I saw the old landlord standing on the porch beside his wife, who sat in a wheelchair. She wore a red woollen hat and a thick muffler around her neck. I admired Eric for peeling fruit with great care for his wife and handing it over to her. Elegantly dressed, Mrs Anderson's appearance appeared respectable. She didn't seem ill at all. How carefully Eric had renovated that old house. He had chopped the logs for the fireplace and piled them up neatly before the fireguard. That day they welcomed us to their home with genuine hospitality. They offered us hot drinks, and we sat in front of the fireplace. I felt happy without thinking that I was troubling them. The older man soon began to play with Danial.

Lugging a toolbox around, Eric always walked around the grounds, fixing things. It seemed to me he had done all the plumbing, the laying out the electric wiring and the carpentry work in the house himself. I always found him doing something around the house, including shovelling the snow off the porch and pathways.

During the next few weeks, Eric and Mrs Anderson strengthened their bonds of friendship with me. His wife taught me how to look after the houseplants. She wanted to know more than anything else about my husband or the father of the baby I was carrying. However, she asked all those questions courteously. Eric soon began to bring us the foods they made using the meat of a deer he had hunted, jams made of raspberries gathered during the summer. They treated Danial in such a way as if he was the only child in the neighbourhood. They kept placing boxfuls of books behind the door of the cottage. I thought there would not be an end to this kindness they showered on us.

Since I arrived in Sweden, hardly anyone has hugged my son. That's why whenever I saw the old couple hugging my son so kindly, I would even become happier than Danial. No sooner would they hear Danial's voice in the grounds than they would, even if they were busy, come out of the house and, resorting to any excuse, they would invite him into their home. I kept saying to myself: 'The winter is coming to an end, and I'll soon give birth to this baby in my belly.'

My telephone contacts with my eternally worried parents made them even more anxious. They kept asking me: 'Have you had your lunch today? Is Danial's digestion all right? You don't sound, right? Has anything happened?' I lied to them that all was going well! But I longed to talk to them, to pour out my heart to them and tell them that I needed them, how things were not right here, and how I was regretting coming here...!

The noose of feeling regretful had coiled around my neck, making me think only about how I had broken my parents' hearts by depriving them of seeing their only grandchild. I remember how my mother wept days and nights after my brother had left. I wanted to return to Iran no matter what. To hell with residency, passport, and America! But I had no identity to return to Iran with – no birth certificate, passport, nothing. So I had no chance of returning. My life now had become a series of regrets, a heap of mistakes for which I had to pay a very high price. I was now seeing myself in the past – the past I had been unable to change. That past had changed me beyond recognition. My mother used to say: 'We can overcome all the afflictions that life throws at us except death!'

My parents could not comprehend that when one leaves one's homeland, it doesn't mean that one has become an alien to the traditions and culture of one's country. On the contrary, one not only becomes more sensitive towards it but shows a keener interest in one's homeland – as a lonely wanderer cast away far from his home which every day finds himself lost in the streets, not knowing where to go.

From time to time, Eric would go to the library in the town and borrow a Teach Yourself Swedish book with a CD for me. He had even found, on occasions, some children's books in Persian for Danial, saying that he mustn't forget his mother language.

One morning I looked out of the window. Everything was covered in snow, looking wonderfully picturesque. So even though my belly was bulging, Danial and I went outside and started to make a snowman. As we got busy,

I saw Eric and his wife, who suddenly came out of the house.

She was in a wheelchair with a thick blanket wrapped around her feet. As Eric began to make a snowball for Danial, she asked me, 'Who looks after you?' I explained that Danial had lost his father and his grandfather and grandmother were not there. Hearing this, she raised her eyebrows and regarded me in dismay as if this was the last straw that broke the camel's back. Then, she said in a nervous tone: 'This must be hard for him. Every child must attend a nursery and a school. This is their right.' Doing my best to appear calm, I replied: 'There's nothing to worry about. As I don't work, I can look after him at home.'

'No. This doesn't seem right,' she said sharply. 'Never mind what you do; this child must play with other children.'

The following morning Eric, Danial, and I went to the nursery in the town. When in there, I didn't know what he was saying to them as he was not talking in his usual calm and articulate manner.

'You realise that this is the right of all the children in this country,' he explained later in Swedish. 'This is not something that we've done for you. It's your child's legal right.'

Hearing him saying all that, I found it impossible to ignore Danial's chance of happiness.

It was two weeks before Danial could stay in the nursery without me. At first, he stepped gingerly into the classroom. Then, I had to sit in a corner and watch him from a distance. He finally settled there.

Eric would also smile whenever he saw Danial playing on the grounds of the house, putting out his arms to hug him. They had become like two old friends. Whenever we paid them a visit, Eric said, 'I'm so happy you came.' Hearing this unexpected welcome would make me stand there stock-still with surprise. My son got used to this kindness quite soon and would tell me: 'Mummy, now I've got a granny and a grandad, haven't I?' Their kindness appeared to be wholly sincere.

'Children must go to bed before eight o'clock in the evening,' Eric would say to me. 'You mustn't allow a child to watch television all day long. This almost amounts to a crime. Furthermore, you're making him isolated at this tender age! His personality will develop best when he spends time with other children.'

The time Eric and his wife spent with Danial had begun to look more normal now. Every day they would ask Danial: 'What did you have for lunch today? Are people nice to you in the nursery?' Is your teacher kind to you?' It had become Eric's habit to ask Danial too many questions. He would listen to all of Danial's childish answers. Now and then, he would tell Danial what a clever boy he was.

I wasn't too curious about their private life. What I mean is that it didn't matter to me if they had any children or grandchildren, why Mrs Anderson was sick, whether she was constantly ill, or what illness she was suffering from! I thought all that wasn't my business.

After dropping Danial in the nursery, I would come home and spend my day in bed until the afternoon, when I would get up and go to pick him up. I would spend most of my time in bed, just like in the days when Sina had left Iran. I felt empty inside. It was as if I was a little white ghost who wandered around without leaving a trace. You would have thought I was invisible in that deserted village. No one would even try to communicate with me except Eric and his wife, who, in all likelihood, thought I was a half-mad or a cruel mother who did nothing for my son. They had asked me repeatedly: 'What do you usually eat? Do you have enough money?' I had tried to tell them that I had sufficient money and that if I ever needed some, my parents would immediately send some cash for me.

'Your son will grow up and will leave you,' my mother told me over the phone. 'Why have you made yourself homeless like this? You could give your son to Isaac's family to look after, and you would finish your degree. Instead, you went to the other side of the world to make yourself and that child unhappy, not to mention us. Believe me, when that child grows up and finds out what you've done to him, he will not even visit your grave.'

'If you're good at a lullaby, why don't you sing it to yourself,' I would reply. 'Why don't you leave me alone now that I've become a woman?'

'A child remains a child for her mother even if she's one hundred years old,' she would sigh.

It was no use arguing with them as they had nothing to do but blame me all the time. Maybe they were right. I was depressed. I kept murmuring some Iranian ditties. I felt like my soul was frozen. It was as if someone had put a lump of ice in my heart. All the time, I was trying to keep my distance from myself. I was under a delusion that if one leaves one's homeland, one would also leave one's fears behind, replacing them with new ones. But that wasn't the case. Everything in my life now had acquired more intensity. I had dragged my past with me, harbouring all the complications of my existence. My fears grew by the minute, making me more depressed. The following days were shrouded in endless darkness, making me feel like I was living in solitary confinement in an eternal, bewildered state of mind.

One late night towards the end of March, I was seized with labour pains. It wasn't that bad at first. Then, all of a sudden, the pain spread to my back, moved to the front and then let go. It suddenly twitched my pelvis, making my intestines ache violently. My head had become heavy, and I let go of a loud shriek. I could only see the whiteness of the ceiling. Danial was babbling in his sleep. I was so worried. What would he do on his own here if I were to die? I felt a cold throbbing along my spinal cord, followed by a sharp spasm. Overcome by terror, I thought, what would happen if I died here? Who will tell the news of my death to my parents? What about Danial? Who would send my corpse to Iran? My father was sick of burial rituals in Iran. I imagined my father, who, after a few days of excitement and the hassle of writing letters to or phoning this official or that, would give up the idea of asking my corpse to be returned to Iran. He did the same with Sina's body. He hated to have anything to do with bureaucrats. I didn't want to get him involved. I tried to call Goli, but her phone was turned off.

I looked for Afshaar's number, but I couldn't find it. I remembered that I had changed my SIM card in Stockholm before I came here. All my numbers had gone. I went to the window. All the lights in Eric's house were off.

The pain eased off a bit. All was quiet. I said to myself I could wait until morning for the first bus. Then, the pain started all over again.

A reddish halo that flickered before my eyes soon turned into a dark, widespread cloud scattered as if by the wind. I typed the name and surname of the biological father in Hitta.se, and after finding his mobile number, I phoned him. He replied with a sleepy voice after my second call. He asked me first to give him my location, which I did at once. The man kept saying: 'Calm down, calm down! We'll be there as soon as we can.'

This was the only reasonable thing I could do. After they arrived, I was asked to sit in the back of the car, which kept jolting and swaying this way and that. Driving recklessly, he didn't give a toss about me. With every jolt of the car, it felt like my intestines were painfully tangled up in my belly.

Once in the hospital, they put me in a wheelchair. A few nurses began asking me question after question: my name, what date I was due, my blood group, whether my waters broke, and if so, when did it happen? How were my labours? How did I give birth to my first baby? Was it a natural or caesarean birth? Did I bleed, and if so, what was the blood's volume and colour? What was the movement of the baby like? When was the last time

I had food? Am I allergic to anything? What medicine have I been taking...? The baby's biological mother hurriedly translated all the answers I screamed out.

I closed my eyes and when I opened them, everywhere was white. I ran my hand over my belly, which had become very flat. They say the most beautiful moment for a woman is when she sees the baby she has given birth to, but I closed my eyes and never saw it. My grandmother used to say, 'Do you know why a child or even a grown-up calm down when they set eyes upon their mother's eyes or cuddle against her? This is because after coming into this world, they feel as if they have left something in their mother's womb, feeling that they've lost something, or that something is missing in their lives.'

Maybe the baby had left something in my womb; one can never tell. Feeling that the baby was stirring, I would keep touching my empty belly. But, no, nothing was there – an empty belly and a weird sort of void. There were still some stains on my nightdress where my waters had broken.

It was as though my body didn't belong to me. My milk kept accumulating in my breasts, and I couldn't tell them to become dry, could I? I wished I could suckle that baby so that there would be no more milk left in my breasts. But every night, I had to empty my very painful breasts.

6

The spring arrived around mid-April. The air was pleasant, as though there had never been a cold and snowy season. Everywhere was so green that it hurt one's eyes. The reflection of the clouds and the trees on the surface of the lake created an enchanting scene. Overcome by ecstasy, the birds thrilled cheerfully, creating a morning symphonic chorus.

Even if I hadn't seen the baby I had carried in my belly, and I guessed I would never see it, I felt sorry for it. This was because I kept crying all the time when it was in my belly. My constant worries and anxieties stopped me from eating nutritious food. I felt conscience-stricken about this neglect. The baby was a girl. I found out about this on the day of my discharge from the hospital – on the white identification wristband was written 'baby girl'. I kept that wristband in my anorak pocket.

There is an old belief in Eastern culture that a newborn can bring either good or bad luck into this world for itself. That little angel turned out to be miraculous for me.

That baby had brought a present for me with her birth. I was sure that this gift came from her. I was finally granted residency, meaning that my asylum application had been successful.

Afshaar had found out where I lived through the baby's biological parents. When I had been hiding from Afshaar and his clique, my solicitor had obtained the court's final decision. Despite the toughening of laws on granting asylum, they had nevertheless made an exception to the rule for the individuals who had handed in their applications before 2014. An added clause in this exception stipulated that individuals who had young babies were exempted from those strict laws and received better treatment. With the perseverance of my solicitor, an acquaintance of Afshaar, I had been granted the highest form of residency – a permanent one.

It was on a Sunday morning that Afshaar came to see me. He had brought me flowers, a box of Iranian cream cakes and a debit card. He said to me with his usual innuendo: 'All the money you left in trust with me plus the down payment kept by Hoshyaar and the last instalment owed you by the baby's parents are in this account. Use this card while sorting out your affairs in the Immigration Office. You can then later open an account for yourself.'

A shiver ran down my spine upon hearing Hoshyaar's name. His repulsive face came to my mind. While he talked, Afshaar tried to bring up the subject of the house and Hoshyaar. I cut him short by saying: 'I don't want to talk about it.'

'We searched for you everywhere,' he continued complaining. 'The parents of this baby were losing their minds. All that time, they kept thinking that maybe something had happened to them and that you or the baby had gone back to Iran. I was caught in all this hassle. After I heard about the good news of your residency, I could only pray that you were still in Sweden.'

'First thing in the morning, you should go to the Immigration Office to sort out your affairs,' Afshaar added. 'Don't forget to wear ironed shoes as you'll have to run from one government department to another. They'll explain everything to you. Contact me if there is any problem or something you cannot understand.'

Afshaar was right. Nearly every week, I had to go to Stockholm to be fingerprinted, take my photo, or go to the General Register Office of the Commune, and...! The rhythm of my life had changed completely. On hearing about my permanent residency, Eric and his wife invited us for supper. They had made a beef roulette with mashed potato and boiled vegetables. I took a bottle of red wine with me.

'Come on, eat up,' Eric kept telling Danial. 'You must eat good food in order to grow up.'

'This supper is given in honour of Danial and you,' Mrs Anderson said contentedly. They soon brought up the subject of what job I was going to do.

'It would be better for Danial if you worked,' they said. I could sense that their kindness was sincere, and I acknowledged my contentment.

'You're most welcome,' Eric said, hugging me. I bent down and hugged Mrs Anderson.

Outside, the silvery crescent of the moon was shining above the row of cypress trees. We both became full after eating the torta cakes.

'I think Eric is your real grandad,' I said to Danial after holding his hand.

'He is,' he yawned.

After a few days, Eric found me an unlooked-for and unusual job. Without delay, he arranged an interview for me in a nursing home. That was the only job I could think of, the sort of job in which I didn't have to deal with hoodlums like Hoshyaar. Eric sorted everything out for me by talking to the manager, an overweight, a handsome elderly lady with short silver hair. She greeted me and went on:

'Your job will not be very complicated. You shall start at eight in the morning from Monday to Friday and finish at four in the afternoon. You'll start your work in the kitchen until you become familiar with the other areas.'

She then introduced me to a middle-aged woman, Anna, who would show me the ropes. Having in mind my little knowledge of Swedish, they spoke calmly and articulately in a polite manner. Next, they handed me a large number of papers and told me I would find all the information I needed.

I was employed immediately as there was a shortage of workers in the district. When I told Afshaar about my job, he said: 'The fact that you have this job is perfect for you until your affairs are sorted. Besides, for you to obtain a visa to go to America, you must have a job; otherwise, they'll not grant you one. You must have been registered in this country's tax system and must have paid your tax. Work for several months and then apply for the visa.'

The days had become longer. Finally, I slowly began to fall into step with Danial's rhythm of walking. I let him poke his head wherever he liked – peer into ants' nests, chase dragonflies, and toss breadcrumbs to the seagulls by the lake.

We would walk for hours beside the lake. Every night I would sit beside Danial and read a story to him. I started learning Swedish because I thought learning another language would be a good hobby. Every day after work, I would ride the bike (that I had bought in a Sunday market with Eric) along the edge of the woods until I would end up where the two sides of the road were nothing but agricultural lands. Further up the road, I would see herds of deer and get so close to them that I could see their brown eyes. The natural landscape was so beautiful that it looked like those pictures in technicolour movies. I would then take one more turn around the area and set off towards the nursery to pick up Danial. I kept telling myself that I would miss that place a lot if I went to America. On second thoughts, though, when in New Jersey, I could go to movies, take holidays, visit a hairdresser to have my hair coloured, meet cheerful people and do lots of other things! The problem was that it took forty-five minutes by car from here to get to the nearest village and about an hour from there to go to the city where we could go, say, to McDonald's or the movies. Nothing much was going on in that village. There were not even buses there during the evenings at weekends. I wanted so badly to visit a large shopping centre or maybe drink coffee or hot chocolate in one of those kiosks in the town centre. I wanted to learn flower arrangements and open a florist shop.

At the beginning of my stay in that village, I knew no one. Then by and by, I came to know many of them. I soon realised that everybody knew everybody else by name and knew all about one another's past. Crossing the village from west to east, you could see only a few streets and doing the same from south to north, you could see fenced-in villas that were mostly summer residences. Beyond the villas, one could see hedged-in agricultural fields of lucerne, wheat, corn, and haystacks.

The trees in front of the nursery were in bud. Yellow, violet, and white flowers had grown on both sides of the road. The apple, pear, and wild cherry trees were in blossom.

The way the village people had begun to react whenever they saw me suggested that I was becoming a more familiar face. It was as though they were curious to find out more about me. They probably wanted to know if I was happy in their country! Feeling contented at my workplace, I got on well with the people there. Even the one who was difficult to please was delighted with me. I never complained about her; she somehow reminded me of my grandmother.

I often felt that I was still pregnant and would touch my belly. I would even feel some pain that I found pretty odd. I would sometimes imagine that the baby's face had features of both of her parents. Most of the time, however, I would try to get rid of those images. Even so, I felt a strange void in my belly. One always feels the absence of something that one once used to have. Of course, you never miss something you never had, something that had never been a part of you. But if you lose something you once had, you will somehow feel its absence.

I had taken up a distance-learning English language course. At the same time, my colloquial Swedish had also improved. One advantage of working with older people is that they talk a lot. So every morning, after dropping Danial off in the nursery, I would go to work. Then, after finishing my career at half-past four, I would go and pick up Danial and do some shopping. Once at home, I would start cooking while he would join Eric, who watered the four o'clock flowers on the grounds. Looking fat and listless, Eric's wife would sit in her wheelchair and watch Danial with sharp eyes, saying: 'Danial is as lively as a flower, isn't he?'

Danial would then follow Eric around in the grounds, who, walking briskly here and there, would prune the branches of an oleander bush with large shears or patiently cut back the branches of a box tree. Eric looked after the grounds, his wife, and Danial as though this was his only occupation. His wife would sit in the sunny part of the grounds and watch.

Eric would make apple pies, and the couple always drank coffee and had cakes on the terrace. Danial, by then, had learned the names of many things, such as birds, flowers, and insects. With its fully-grown leaves, the vine bush had crept up the trellis, casting a shade onto the garden. The garden was full of dog-roses, roses, snapdragons, and geraniums. The aroma of jasmine filled the air. It had been years since I had smelled the scents of those flowers. Seeing Eric working in his garden reminded me of my dad. The latter would spend all the spring and summer afternoons watering the flowers in our garden, filled with the smell of delicious foods my mother cooked. Maybe the main reason my dad never emigrated to America was the scent of those jasmines and the ceramic hawz in the middle of the courtyard. He said, 'One cannot take his house with him to another country.'

After telling my family about the news of my residency, my mother was happier than anyone else.

'As soon as you arrive in America, we'll join you there,' she said. 'We'll go to Turkey soon and apply for a visa to America. I've had enough of your father's shilly-shallying. Even if he doesn't want to come, I'll look after Danial. After that, you can do whatever pleases you – traveling with your cousins, for example.'

My parents could only come to Sweden when I had obtained Swedish citizenship, after which I could send them an invitation letter. But, unfortunately, that was only possible after four years of continuously living here.

I missed my parents. It was as though my life with them was a different kind of life. Everything was always prepared for me – I had my room, my food was always ready, and my mother made fresh fruit juice every morning. My parents looked after me for days when I had a slight cold or other illness. Here I had become another person who had no resemblance to her former existence. You would have said I had become a mature woman, ready to bloom. I wanted to be myself, what I was and had been before.

Goli came to see me now and then. She was happier than anyone else that I had obtained permanent residency. Every time she came to see me, she brought a gift for Danial. When I told her how expensive the gift was, she said, 'Look. I've found a good, full-time job in a boutique, earning better wages now. Very soon, I'll move into a larger flat.' I had made a cake for Danial's birthday, and Goli had bought five candles and a paper hat. I had also invited Eric and his wife to the celebration.

'Let's go to the city one day and look around,' she whispered in my ear when we were in the kitchen. 'You'll soon go crazy here! These people can look after your son for a day.'

'I like the idea, but I feel a bit shy to ask them,' I replied while I was washing the dishes and Goli was frying the asparagus and the chicken.

'No worries!' she said. 'They'd be pleased. But don't you see how lonely they are?'

'You're right; they are lonely,' I said, placing the lettuce leaves in the bowl and arranging the small tomatoes. 'But I'd be worried about Danial, who may not cope without me!'

'For how long are you going to live like this?'

'Until I leave this place,' I answered, pouring the corn from the tin onto the salad. 'Why don't you go out with anyone live then? Not having a child, you could easily meet someone, couldn't you?'

'I've hit upon an interesting idea,' she said, placing the chicken beside the asparagus on a large platter. 'I'm sick and tired of looking for one man with everything I want.

So instead, one should be with three men simultaneously – one would be handsome and athletic just for sex, the other a middle-aged rich man from whose bank account one can draw cash, and the third one should be a lovesick romantic.'

I wondered if Danial, looking for some cake in the kitchen, understood what we were talking about.

I think you mean steamy, dampened, and feverish?' I said under my breath.

'Spot on!' she agreed.

We both laughed out so loud that Eric and his wife were surprised. He stood up and peeped inside the kitchen to see what was happening.

7

It was before dusk on a rainy day towards the end of May. Danial's pieces of Lego were scattered all over the floor. The night-lamp on the windowsill was casting a pale light into the room. Outside the window, the blossoms on the apple tree were dripping with rain. Not a sound could be heard outside. I looked out of the window. A man was standing on the ground talking to Eric. I had never seen him before in the village. I could see his profile clearly under the lamp on the floor. He had white skin, and his golden hair was combed back. I didn't know who he was or what he wanted.

The following day I sat on the bench in the yard with a cup of coffee in my hand. It was a cloudless day, and the sun's heat was pleasant. The scent of snowberry flowers and the box trees filled the air. All the trees had blossomed with white flowers. Not a leaf was stirring on the trees in the woods immediately behind the villa. One could only hear the noise made by Danial, who was playing with the mud, pebbles, and sand in front of the building. He kept heaping the sand onto a toy lorry, only to empty it again while making different sounds.

The sound of a car skidding on the gravel road was heard from a distance. An all-terrain Volvo was driven straight on to the grass on the grounds. Seeing the car, Danial stopped what he was doing and followed it with his eyes until it came to a halt in front of Eric's house. The same man talking to Eric in the yard the night before got out of the car.

At that moment, Eric appeared from behind the building in old working clothes and with shears in his hand. The man turned and looked at Danial and smiled. Seeing me standing there, he eyed me in such a way as if he had seen an alien in broad daylight. He walked up to me, put out his hand with a brave smile, and introduced himself. I felt the palm of his hand, which was filthy, with the skin flaking off. I could only respond with apprehension. I didn't even manage to catch his name. Once he turned to talk to Eric, I saw the bald patch at the back of his head.

I immediately went back into the cottage, dropped onto the sofa, and remained there motionless – something I frequently did. I began reading a book from where I had left without concentrating. I felt so weak that I could hardly get on my feet if it weren't for Danial.

I borrowed that book from the library. It was a book by Virginia Woolf translated into Persian. I hesitated on these lines: 'Without your presence, the colours of life fade away. I am still there, dried-up and dusty, like a drop of water squeezed out of a sponge and fallen on the ground...!'

Hearing Danial's voice outside, I stood up and peeped out of the window at the man still standing there. He appeared to be an ordinary, middle-aged man of average build and medium height, and nothing was attractive about him. I couldn't guess his age – around forty or maybe more. I pulled on a V-neck white top with black Adidas jogging bottoms and trainers. Before leaving, I brushed my hair and looked at myself in the mirror near the entrance door.

Having looked at my face in the mirror countless times, I had noticed how tight my lips had become. I knew more than anyone else how much I had lost touch with my inner self.

I went out of the cottage. The sun was shining. The man stood beside Danial, playing with the pebbles and the sand; as I walked towards them, the man squatted down and started talking to Danial.

'It looks like you're making a castle!' he said.

With childish seriousness, Danial looked at the heap of pebbles and sand he had made, probably not sure what he had made. 'Where is he from?' the man asked me with a smile as if he didn't want to ask him directly.

'Iran,' I answered.

'*Yaa-Allah*,' he shook his head.

'We speak Persian,' I corrected him. '*Yaa-Allah* is Arabic.'

At that moment, Eric joined us and began to chat with Danial.

'Let's go to the woods,' I told Danial in Persian.

We took the pathway in the woods opposite our house. Lined on both sides of the path were a significant number of beech trees, the roots of some of which stuck out from the soil. We had hardly gone far from the house when I heard footsteps behind me. Overcome by fear, I stopped.

'Hey,' I heard his manly voice behind me, which made me start. Then, seeing that I looked shocked, he said politely: 'I'm sorry if I scared you.'

'Not at all,' I said, shaking my head.

'Can I accompany you?' he said with a smile.

I agreed. He looked at me admiringly in a naïve manner. That was what I was after. I thought, why not give it a go and let him walk beside me? I just listened as he quite soon began to talk. Finally, he stopped walking and asked me: 'By the way, do you understand what I'm saying?' I couldn't understand half of what he was saying. I smiled stupidly.

'I can speak in English if you'd find it easier,' he suggested.

'I'd rather talk in Swedish,' I said.

'All right, I'll start over again,' he said. 'You can stop me when you don't understand, and I'll speak slowly. How long have you been here?'

'About two years.'

'Do you work here?'

I suddenly felt I had gotten myself into a fix. I didn't want to go on talking. I slowed down and stopped walking for a moment. Noticing my silence, he stopped asking me further questions. He then started to admire Danial, who was running ahead of us. Finally, we arrived at a pond surrounded in a semicircle by tall trees.

Danial kept poking a stick into the ants' nests. We sat down on a bench. He smelled pleasant. On the other side of the pond was grassland that could be seen through the trees. He started once more talking about himself. He spoke in an agreeable manner that didn't bore me at all. His masculine voice rang pleasantly in my ears. He then fell silent and cast a sidelong glance at me as though he waited to hear me say something. Not daring to say anything, I remained quiet. On the way back, the pathway was deserted.

When we were close to the cottage, he stopped and said, after a pause: 'It's very nice these days. It's good to be out and about. The air in the house gets too hot. I'll pick you up tomorrow morning at ten. I can show you up there.' He then pointed out the other side of the village, adding: 'There are many lakes in this region, and I can show you all the nooks and crannies here.' All of a sudden, a long-suppressed joy was rekindled in me. How he looked at me had a warmth I had not felt for a long time.

I woke up early the following day. I had a shower and put the kettle on. I decided from that day to do my daily exercise! I stood before the mirror and looked at myself from every possible angle. I hadn't put on much weight. Once again, I looked like I did when I wasn't pregnant. It was nine o'clock, and Danial was still asleep. I had to wake him up before that man came!

I picked some flowers from the space between the cottage and the woods and put them on the table. I switched on the radio. My favourite singer Sting was singing (Every Breath You Take), a song he sang during the eighties.

Around a quarter to ten, the man appeared outside the cottage door in his tracksuit. When I opened it, he showed me the muffins he had bought and then waited in the hallway. I felt he was acting as if he didn't want to be a nuisance. But, on the other hand, he also seemed to be imposing himself on me. I offered him a cup of coffee, and he entered the sitting room relaxed. No sooner had I nipped into the kitchen than he followed me and stood before me. Gazing at me, he sat down on a chair. Then, pointing his hand at a place outside, he said: 'I live in a house opposite the church. I'm going to stay there for a while.'

I poured out another coffee for him. He took a piece of the muffin. I wanted to say something, but I didn't dare. He was quiet too. While drinking his coffee, he said, out of the blue:

'I'm known in the village because of my grandfather, who used to live here. He was called Andreas, and my name is Andreas Johan.'

Danial had woken up by now and was playing with his iPad. We could hear him in his room jumping around and a monotonous sound coming from his computer.

I could see the man trying to find a subject to resume his talking. Then, finally, he stood up and washed his cup in the sink. He then asked me to hand him my cup, which he began to flow.

'It's very quiet here,' he said.

'Too quiet!'

'I need some peace and quiet away from the crowd, away from any kind of noise,' he went on. 'All you can hear in this place is the sound of seagulls. What's the population of Iran, by the way?'

'Around eighty million.'

'Wow!' he said, whistling quietly.

From the questions he asked about Iran, I gathered he didn't know much about my homeland. He thought Iran was a salt-desert land in which nothing grew and where all the men wore Arabic clothes and all the women walked around in burqas. I tried to explain to him that Iran is not an Arabic country. The only things we had in common with Arabic countries were the oil and Islam and the fact that Iranians descended from the Indo-Arian or even the Arian race!

'Does it matter to you where we come from on this planet?' he said, shaking his head. 'Have you ever heard about the concept of a global village?'

I found the subject of conversation interesting but being afraid of him asking too many questions that I couldn't answer, I quickly put Danial's clothes on, made a bread-and-butter sandwich for him, put it in the bag, and the three of us went out.

It was sunny and warm. Barbeques and table tennis were set up in the space outside the house with many bicycles. The people in the village were busy grilling and drinking beer. We passed the school on the left-hand side of the square and the church directly opposite the school. He told me that he had been baptised in that church and showed me the house in which his grandfather's friends used to live and the restaurant, now closed, which had been his grandfather's hang-out in bygone years. All along the way, he talked about his childhood and youth. The fact that I had no memories with any people here to share with him made me sad.

'Did you have a happy childhood?' he then asked me.

I nodded affirmatively. He began to tell me some things about his life – his business trip to Japan, his recent divorce, his nine-year-old and seven-year-old daughters, and how the younger one knew by heart the names of all the capital cities. I noticed a slight tremble when he talked about his daughters. He then spoke about his parents, who brought him here to spend his summer holidays while they went back to Stockholm to get on with their jobs. After that, he went on to talk about countless other subjects. I felt something more was going on between him and me; otherwise, what was the point of him trying to share his childhood memories with me?

We kept walking in the village while he showed me the landmarks from his childhood. Finally, he ran his hand over the trunk of an ancient oak tree in the middle of the village and said: 'Did you know that this tree has been here for hundreds of years?'

We wanted to go into the graveyard, but its gate was closed. We continued walking. The fact that the chance of visiting the graves of Sina, grandmother, or even Isaac was taken away from me made me feel downhearted. I didn't even know whether I could ever attend my parents' funerals.

Danial, having become bored, wanted to play. So that's why we went to the park beside the church, and Johan started to play with Danial by putting him on a swing. With every push of the swing, Danial flew higher and higher so that I thought he might fly up to the clouds. But, being happy, Danial kept laughing, and that was all I wanted.

Using a different excuse every day, Johan visited us for about a week. It had become as clear as daylight that I wanted to be happy. A feeling of joyfulness had arisen in my soul. His every smile and accidental touch made me quiver with pleasure. I felt optimistic thinking about what was about to come. I would sit beside the window and let the air from the woods caress my face. This was the only fun I had here. Secretly, I wished he would show up again. However, I had nothing to do but stand in front of the mirror, beautify myself, wear my colourful dresses, dry my hair with the hair-dryer, and finally put deep-red lipstick on so that he wouldn't find out how sad I was! During our walks with Danial, we would stop every now and again and watch a playful squirrel leaping from branch to branch or a crow swooping down noisily to steal a seed. While we walked along the narrow pathways among wild plants, watching out for snakes, I felt I was living again. Enjoying life in moments like this, I rediscovered tranquillity and the experience of being close to someone.

Pronouncing his words, Johan would speak slowly when he talked to me. Sometimes he would read my lips and, at the same time, articulate my words after listening to them. We had long, pleasant conversations. He would sometimes cast a meaningful glance at me and smile, which meant he thought I was stupid.

He would often laugh by making fun of me when I mispronounced some words. I would, for example, mix up 'cage' with 'box.' In the Swedish language, many words are written similarly, and only a different accent on a letter can change the meaning of a word. That week I had started with a novel enthusiasm to learn how to use verbs in Swedish – regular and irregular. There are more irregular verbs in Swedish than regular ones.

We had not had any physical contact until the day when we lay beside one another on the grassland. His closeness to me on the grass filled me with a longing to make love to him. With his arms lifted, Danial was running along the edge of the woods at the end of the grassland. I sat up and shouted at him in Farsi: '*Bargard*. It's dangerous!'

'What's the meaning of '*Bargard*'?' Johan asked and repeated, '*Bargard, bargard*. You can teach me Persian, and I'll be your Swedish teacher. *Bargard*!'

Johan got to his feet and helped me by holding my hand, which he kissed. Then, clasping my hand, he put it into his trouser pocket, not letting go of it along the way. Finding that tender gesture incredible, my heart nearly missed a beat.

My instinct told me that the friendship I had been waiting for since my arrival in Sweden had happened. The scenery was lovely, and as I walked, the image of Sina came to my mind for some unknown reason.

'You look so much like my brother,' I said gently.

You told me you were the only child! I don't want to talk about him right now.' I heaved a long sigh.

On Saturday, he took me in his car to the city. We went into a café, and after standing at the bar, we sat at a small table. Two young men with strange long hair with a guitar standing beside them were seated at another table, talking in hushed voices. A man and a woman were sitting at a table near the window, whispering to one another.

During those hours with him that day, I experienced the sweetness of happiness in all my being. As the café was getting warm, we sat at a table in the sun above us in that afternoon hour. It was pleasant to drink cold beer in the glistening, golden rays of the sun.

He looked at me sideways when his leg accidentally touched mine under the table. He then put his cold hand between my thighs. I looked into his eyes and smiled. He told me that during the first month after his separation from his wife, he had spent nearly every night in the bistros in the city, going to bed completely drunk. He then talked, trying hard to explain many things to me. Finding myself empathising with him, I realised he needed someone to pour out his heart. He saw me as someone from a different planet to whom he could quickly unburden his inner feelings and thoughts. He knew I was not the person to judge him or abuse what he had told me. From how he looked at me, I could see that he trusted me wholeheartedly. Finally, he went into the café to order two more drinks.

'What perfume are you wearing?' he asked me, putting the drinks on the table.

'Why do you ask?' I said. 'Does it remind you of someone?'

'Nobody,' he answered. 'This is a unique scent that only belongs to *you*.' He added, 'Did you know that scientists have discovered that people fall in love with each other because of their unique scents.'

His emphasis on the word *you* was such that I suddenly felt reassured. I began to pour out the terms one after another, not caring how to use verbs, adverbs, or where to put *en* or *ett*. I only told him why I was in Sweden. I explained to him that I was a Jew and had never had any plans of coming here. I was an asylum seeker hoping to join my relatives in America as soon as possible. I told him about all the difficulties I had had here. I told him that Isaac had just disappeared and we couldn't find his corpse. I also told him how my father-in-law's house, where I had stayed after my husband's death, had turned into a prison where, grief-stricken, I kept hitting my head against the walls like a blind bird. I never mentioned anything about Hoshyaar or the man with the pram. I told him I had never planned how to live and that my life had always been like this – a shadow of a gigantic question mark cast eternally everywhere over my life.

Maybe it was not unusual for someone like me, who had not had a proper conversation with anyone, to gabble like that. I felt happy that I could talk so comfortably and calmly like that. Johan responded so kindly and wisely to my story that I couldn't believe a man could listen with genuine interest to what I was saying. He reminded me of my brother.

He raised his eyebrows as a sign of surprise, a gesture that I found quite pleasant. I had thought before that he would have run away from me if I had told him about my situation. Instead, the sentence he murmured in my ear is so carved in my memory that I will never forget it: 'My Iranian princess, I will look after you.'

After hearing this, I burst out quietly weeping, not knowing why. He closed his inflamed eyelids through which ran two greyish-purple capillary vessels. A wrinkled line appeared in the middle of his forehead, showing that he was sunk into deep thought. We both remained quiet. Leaning towards me, he put his hands around my lower waist so that I felt he was holding me from my waist. He put my head against his shoulder, lowered his head, and kissed my eyes which I let him do. He then gently kissed my lips. Withdrawing my head as a protest sign, I whimpered, 'Ey!'

Ignoring my protest, he kissed me passionately. I closed my eyes. This was the first time someone had kissed me in a public place.

I had come from a land where kissing and cuddling in public was considered a crime! Maybe it was because of these differences between the two cultures that I felt there, and then something had happened to me; something beyond mere friendship, something akin to a miracle. So put, I had fallen in love.

I shouldn't in any way think that what brought the two of us together was a pure coincidence. Not having perhaps felt like this before, I was happy. He seemed to be very kind and was exceptionally kind to Danial. He must have been the same with his children. I had become once again that mischievous little girl whose knees were continuously grazed. Now he was the one who cared not about my injured knees but my wounded soul. Feeling as though he had taken my brother's place, I felt calm beside him.

After returning to the village, he drove the car to his grandfather's house. No lights could be seen behind the windows. We passed across the yard and went behind the house.

'I've got a magic box for Danial,' he said, turning to Danial. 'Promise you'll play carefully with it and put everything in the right place once you've finished playing. Promise?'

Danial nodded affirmatively. 'Would you like to come to the basement with me?' he asked. 'My grandfather used to hide the basement keys somewhere. Aha, I've found them.'

The keys were hidden under a large flower-pot. He opened the door, which made a creaking noise. After stepping on the first step of the staircase, he turned and held my hand. Danial stood in the doorway.

'Come down,' he said, carefully holding my hand. We stood there for a moment. He switched on the torch and said: 'Come and see my boxful of books here.'

The dark basement was barely lit, with only a gleam of light from outside. The air was filled with wood and the musty smell of naphthalene.

'Look,' he said after picking up a book from the box. '*The Old Man and the Sea*.'

'I read this book when I was a child,' I said, smiling.

'When you were a child?' he said, surprised.

'My brother had this book.'

Another book that he showed me was *Moby Dick*. I found it quite uncanny what Isaac and Johan had in common. Sina was always reading *Moby Dick*. I will never forget the picture on its cover. However, *Moby Dick* never interested me. To me, it was like *The Adventures of Tintin* – a wholly boyish book. How strange both of them were! As if trying to remember something, he looked around thoughtfully and, after finding a wooden box, said: 'Here it is. I've found it.'

The box was full of soldier figures which his grandfather kept as souvenirs of the Second World War. Taking so much pride in keeping those figures, he became overexcited like a little kid. He then said to Danial: 'Danial, you're the only one I will let play with these toys!'

Seeing those toy soldiers, Danial became excited and kept asking to hold the box in his hands. But Johan said: 'No. You must wait!' After handing the box to Danial, he added, 'We can all go to my house, and I'll show you my photo album while Danial plays with his toys. No, I'll make a special dinner for you that we can have with my old wine. What do you say?'

Upon hearing this, I blushed, and feeling ill-at-ease, I hesitated a bit. However, when I nodded my consent, he was in rapture. Once outside his house, he held Danial's hand and entered, and I followed them. It was a villa with three bedrooms decorated with chinaware, carpeted with threadbare rugs and trinkets that had been collected for many years. On the mantelpiece, I could see the framed photo of an older man wearing traditional clothes and military boots standing alongside his horse beside the sizeable main gate of their mansion house.

'My grandfather was a military man,' Johan said, pointing to the picture. 'He wanted me to be a military man, just like him.'

I suddenly remembered that I hadn't asked him what he did for a living. First, he went into the bedroom to change his clothes. Then, he strode back into the dust-covered sitting-room, wearing a white T-shirt, pair of short trousers, and sandals. He had also combed his sparse hair to one side and dabbed some cologne on his neck. When I asked him what his job was, he replied with a smile: 'It's interesting you ask me that question now. They first ask you what you do for a living, how much you earn each month, and where you live. But you have never asked me that question until now.'

'These things do not matter to me,' I said. 'These things do not define human beings.'

Johan nodded as a sign of agreement and talked a little about his job. He was the manager of a research project working on architectural structures.

We had dinner at a large table in the sitting-room. The balcony window was wide open, letting in the pleasant air from outside. After frying a fresh fish, he garnished it with some prawns, added a mixture of honey, vinegar, and herbs, and put the dish on the table. When I offered my help, he motioned to sit down, telling me he had always cooked for his wife and children. Then, he poured some wine for me, added a brandy to his glass, and said: 'Cheers!'

He had stylishly decorated the table. Half asleep, Danial rolled over on the sofa facing the television. I yawned. He asked me: 'Are you tired?' He got up, shut the balcony window, and said: 'It has started to rain.'

He fetched two blankets from the bedroom. He spread one of them over Danial and said: 'Children are such lovely creatures!' He threw the other one over my legs, saying: 'You must be cold!'

He lit the lamp on the windowsill, and it all looked romantic. He poured some more wine into our glasses. There was silence for a long time except for the sound of his breathing.

'Come and sit beside me,' he said quietly.

Seeing me not budging, he came and sat beside me. I looked at him and smiled. He kissed my lips, and I kissed his forehead. He began to play with his fingers with a lock of hair curled behind my ear. He sniffed suddenly, and then I saw his tears dropping on my left hand. With that hand, I wiped away his tears. Seeing him weep like that, I became breathless. I tried to raise his head, but he said: 'Shush, shush!'

'Don't, please!' I said.

'Don't say anything, don't ask anything!'

I kissed him hard on the lips. I took his glass of wine and nestled his head against my chest as I did to Danial whenever he cried. My top became wet with his tears. I could hear the raindrops drumming rhythmically against the windowpane.

I felt he was my kindred soul – someone like Sina. He had somehow suffered a lot, being one of those human beings who had endured pain and heartache. He then fell into prolonged silence, looking at me with eager eyes. Finally, he helped me by taking my hand and leading me to the bedroom. We lay on the bed beside one another. He then gently kissed me with a lingering one. Finally, I could hold my breath no longer. Gazing into my eyes, he clutched my breasts, put his tongue into my mouth, opened my legs wide, and lay on me.

As I tried to undress, he said: 'Stay as you are. I'm happy like this.'

He continued to kiss me. Suddenly he took my clothes off with incredible force and made me sit on him. Not having made love for such a long time, I felt so much pain that I thought I was about to lose my virginity again. He kept pressing his head against my neck, saying all the time: 'Oh, my darling, my darling, I hope you're not in pain?'

'No,' I kept saying, raising my head.

I was always worried about not waking Danial by making any noise. He whispered to me to ensure I kept quiet: 'Shush, shush!' I rested my head on his hairless chest. His nipples were as hard as two unopened buds, and he had a hard-on.

Taking turns closing our eyes for some minutes, we listened to one another's breathing until morning. He kept saying to me: 'Your large eyes shine in the dark!'

It was incredible that no one had mentioned anything about my body heat so far, but Johan noticed it. He was right; my body was always scorching, particularly during sleep. We cuddled one another whenever one of us woke up. Resuming our lovemaking all over again, he slipped his penis into me. Already moist, I became even wetter. He would then pour more wine into his glass. We cared about each other during our lovemaking. He moved on my body like coming and going waves. I kept clawing at the sheets, biting the edge of the pillow, panting, and moaning with pleasure.

It was around daybreak when he awoke, raising his head from between my legs and looking at me with blue eyes glistening like stars.

'No man had ever made..., like...,' I murmured.

After wiping his mouth with the back of his hand, he kissed me hard again.

Your eyes are blue,' I said.

No, they're not blue,' he said. 'They're grey.'

'No, they're blue.'

'No, I told you they're grey.'

I looked around. The bedroom window looked out into the woods. The scents of the woods and the lake from outside drifted into the room, mingling with the smell of our bodies.

'You're mine now, aren't you?' he said, looking at me gravely, and stretching his body.

'I think so,' I said, rubbing my eyes with my hands.

'You're so beautiful!' he said, kissing me simultaneously.

When he wanted to get up, I grabbed his hand, kissed him gently, closed my eyes, and said: 'Stay a bit longer beside me. I want to sleep more.'

'You sleepyhead!' he said. 'You have some rest. I'll give Danial his breakfast.'

He left the room and shut the door behind him. I wanted to stay in bed the whole day. I could hear him playing with Danial. Opening my eyes later, I found a tray on which was placed a bouquet of pansies with a note beside it written by Johan that read: 'Thank you for last night.'

'What's the time?' I asked.

'About midday.'

I stretched out my arms and hugged him. Then, having entered the bedroom, Danial jumped up and down on the bed, and Johan was as happy as a kid.

'How I love your smile in the morning,' he said and asked Danial: 'Would you like to go for a swim?' He then told me: 'It's sunny. We could all go for a swim. Danial and I might even do some fishing.'

***

Johan jumped off the boardwalk into the lake and swam a long distance. He was showing off to me. I laughed as he pushed back his sparse hair. The sun was burning the backs of my legs, making me look tanned due to the colour of my skin. His mobile phone in his trousers' pocket started to ring, so I motioned to him that it was ringing. Looking worried, he quickly came out of the water, took out the mobile with his wet hands, and walked far away from me. I watched him as he talked rapidly, waving his hand. He walked up and down a few times.

'Is everything all right?' I asked him when he would come back.

'Yes, everything is OK,' he said and poured me some coffee from the flask.

Further away, a woman was pulling a dog's leash that kept barking. I wasn't sure whether I should trust him or not. But having trusted him already, I felt good about

it and victorious. I saw the same thing in his eyes in the
way he looked at me.

'Don't you think it's a miracle that two people find
one another the way we've done in this topsy-turvy
world?' he kept saying.

By and by, I realised that life wasn't about
daydreaming; I could be happy with this man. We
talked all the time whenever we were together. I could
easily forget all about my horrible experiences when I
was with him. Having come to the end of my rope
before I met Johan, I had almost run out of the will to
go on living.

My mother had always wished to find a husband for
me who was a doctor so that she could ask his advice
about her occasional headaches that she attributed to
migraine. I knew she wanted a son-in-law who could
replace her lost son.

'I thought he would be a much healthier-looking
man,' she complained after seeing Johan's face on a
video-call. 'How old is he?'

'Maman, Swedish people are very pale with fair
eyebrows that make them look a bit sickly,' I explained
to her. 'But they're generally much healthier than us.'

When I told Johan he was the second man in my life
with whom I had slept; he wouldn't believe me.
Counting on his fingers, he told me he had slept with

ten women. He talked about his relationships in such a way as though he had no regrets and had done whatever he liked.

'I don't care how many women you've slept with in the past,' I told him. 'But you see, I'm a jealous woman, and from now on....'

'I'm even more jealous!' he said, cutting me short. 'You're perfectly within your rights to be with anyone you like. Sweden is the land of freedom and democracy. But you must promise me that you would let me know if you were to meet someone else. What I mean is that you would first finish with me.'

'But you don't have any right to finish with me to find someone else,' I said.

'How can I find anyone like you in this world?'

He bit my cheek, causing me pain, and I nearly screamed. Finally, he held my head between his hands and breathed his warm breath on my hair, pressing me so hard against himself that I could hardly breathe.

We were bound to one another by an eternal power. We never became tired of each other. We spent every day of June and July together. What was incredible was that he could spend the whole night and the day after in bed, making love to me. I found being with him made me feel feminine. He had something in him that filled up the void in my existence. I felt as though talking to him opened the pores in my skin, making it breathe. Having become an inseparable part of my days, he soon became my life's beating heart.

I don't know how I have lived all those years on my own without him. I loved him so much that I didn't want to lose him at any cost. Talking about ordinary subjects, we often ended up, by free association, telling one another about our unique childhood memories. Our being together was like having free-of-charge psychoanalysis sessions. By going over our recollections, we recounted the ups and downs that helped us to soothe our pains.

I felt like I was floating like a small cloud in the sky. For the first time since I came to this country, I could see a peaceful future ahead of me. I drew the curtain away to let the daylight in, and I looked at his face while he was asleep. He looked paler in the light cast on his face. The fresh air from outside mingled with his body odour in the room. My hands smelt of his body and his penis. Even my breath had the smell of his penis. I went into the bathroom, brushed my teeth, put on my earrings from the Qajar period given to me by my grandmother, and put on some red lipstick. I put my hair up, washed my body in the warm water, and went back to bed without putting on my nightgown and lay beside him. When my leg touched him, he turned over and hugged me.

'I want to make love again,' I said, smiling after kissing him.

He laughed and pulled the duvet over my head.

We had become so close to one another that we felt breathless. The rhythm of our love-making was becoming more intense by the day. Our love for each other was so profound that we thought neither of us would ever leave the other. Those days were the best days of my life, and I didn't care where I lived in this world as long as I was in this happy paradise.

He would often enthrall me by telling me stories of his life and that he had spent most of his summers in this village. The photo of his tall grandfather in his military outfit looked much like him, with Johan sharing only a little of that man's military resoluteness. Compared to his grandfather, Johan was a remaining caricature of a long-forgotten ancestor. Having a delicate and easily-hurt soul, he looked sad most of the time, and as though having taken his mother's place, I looked after him. Sulking sometimes for no reason, I had to caress him for hours, kiss him on the brow and give him a good hug.

He would tell me stories he had heard in his childhood, including reports of ghosts that wandered in the village. Being a natural story-teller, his tales transported me to a magical world such that I couldn't tell whether it was real or imaginary. His voice, in all probability, was the best weapon in his story-telling armoury that had remained silent for years. He had me many times that neither his wife nor his children had visited that village region. Having unusual qualities, his voice was capable of producing high-pitched and bass sounds. Hearing him talk, I could comprehend the soul of the Swedish language. I never knew a language was capable of having a soul. The Swedish language has a lovely melody to it. The tone of Johan's voice, when telling stories, was always something between soft and hard notes. He let the words sink into my mind. It was a confused babble of sounds and syllables that needed time for the different obscure messages to find their proper places for me to grasp their meaning. As my ears became used to hearing those strange sounds hidden in the new language, the words began to do their jobs.

I grabbed my mobile, and we began to look for the music on YouTube. As he began to murmur the poems of Tomas Tranströmer, he kept telling me: 'Now you sing with me. You must sing. Repeat once more. Sing softly and clearly.' He would then ask me: 'Do you understand their meaning?' I would show with an upward jerk of my head that I didn't understand!

'I only understand you,' I would say. 'I understand your body.' Come to think of it, how had I found a man with the moral qualities we had in common.

'You're like a miracle that has happened in my life,' I kept saying to him loudly.

'No, listen. You're the miracle in my life,' he would say. 'Here's my village in which my grandfather lived. Here's where I was born and being with you here is the best thing that has happened to me. With your dark hair and eyes like those of a frightened gazelle, you have a genuine Semitic face. Even better, you are like a Persian carpet with intricate, beautiful patterns that make one imagine faraway exotic places. No, no, what am I saying? You are like a colourful stained-glass window that transports one to those far-off times in the Middle Ages when one's imagination wanders in Elysium Fields.'

I loved it when he talked like that.

'You don't know much about him yet,' Goli said one day. 'You don't know who he is. Has he ever introduced you to his daughters and relatives? Give it some time until you get to know each other better. Have you ever checked his mobile? Why doesn't he answer his mobile in front of you? You told me this yourself.'

She was right. He would only answer his mobile after walking some distance away from me, and then I would see him talk rapidly to someone. But I had never listened to his conversations and tried to eavesdrop on what he was saying a few times. So I hadn't understood anything.

'Stop it, Goli, will you!' I said to her. 'What does a woman want in life? He has all the qualities I've always wished for in a man I can live with. But, the most important thing is the love he shows to Danial and me.'

There was no point in arguing with Goli as she held men in total contempt, dismissing them all with one sweep. Having made up my mind, I wasn't prepared in any way to leave him – this man who had accompanied me all along, who would kiss my neck, making me feel attractive. I felt in my bones that I looked beautiful and felt feminine once again; it was as though all my hormones were balanced. How could I make Goli understand that I felt like a real woman by being with Johan?

Everything had started rapidly to get better.

'Your invitation letter is ready,' my uncle told me on the phone. 'All you have to do is make an appointment with the American Embassy. The Jewish Society here will support you, including paying for your plane ticket. Only you need to hurry up, dear!'

One night as we were sitting on the sofa looking out of the window, he asked me: 'Would you like some wine?'

He then went into the kitchen and returned with two glasses of wine. I noticed that he was avoiding eye contact with me. Then, I saw a flock of larks in the sky that changed direction and flew away. The evening sky was as violet as jasmines.

'Wherever you go, the sky is the same colour,' my grandmother said. But I had never seen a sky the colour of jasmine-violet.

Danial was absorbed in playing with the toy cars that Johan had bought. Then, making hooting sounds, he joined the vehicles, one behind the other. He then put each car on the lift, tossing them down the slope.

Johan stretched his body and sat beside me.

'I must go back to Stockholm,' he said with a heavy sigh. 'I can't stay here any longer. What do you think? Would you like to come with me? You can move in with me.'

He moved closer to me and nestled his head against my neck, and said: 'This is my usual favourite spot.'

He knew exactly where to put his head where my pulse throbbed. I could feel the beating of his heart in my chest.

'I can picture us growing old together, sitting for hours in front of the television, you are bringing me my pills and herbal infusions,' he continued. 'I'll then ask you to put on that blue top with the violet flowers, and

I'll rest my head in the usual place on your shoulder. Just imagine. I don't ever want to lose you, ever. After my children, you're the dearest one, and I worship you. I don't wish any harm to come to you. That's why I have to ensure your future will be provided for. I promise I'll look after your child just like my own. I've been thinking a lot during our time together. I've concluded that I cannot live without you. I need you. You must come and live with me.'

I put my hand on his head and stroked it, taking a deep breath and gulping down his body odour. I closed my eyes like a blind person who touched something for the first time to find out what it was.

'Would you like us to get married in a church or a synagogue?' he went on. 'Why don't I take you to Saint Maurice Church? No. Wait. Why don't we go to Stockholm?'

'Why are you asking me all this?' I asked.

'You see, I'm sick and tired of all these present-day women,' he said. 'All they do is try to prove how superior they are. You're very different from them.'

'Maybe it's because I believe there's nothing to prove about anything,' I said. 'I don't believe in anything, let alone try to prove it.'

'I'd like to marry you and register it somewhere,' he said, standing up and looking into my eyes. 'What do you think?'

'Marriage?' I exclaimed.

'In what language do you want us to get married? Hebrew, Farsi, or Swedish?'

'If you want to marry me, you'll have to be circumcised first.'

'Really?' he said, glancing at his penis.

'Positive,' I said. 'Otherwise, it can't be done,' I went on, pulling his leg. Then, grabbing his penis, I said: 'They'll only chop off just a little bit of the tip of the hanging skin. Then, after the operation, you must wear a long loincloth until your bits are healed!'

Terrified and flabbergasted, he looked at his penis. We both laughed heartily.

'Idiotic, isn't it?' I said.

'It is. Let's forget that!' he said. 'Would you like to get married in a church or a synagogue?'

'It makes no difference to me where in the world I get married,' I replied. 'I don't believe in any speech made anywhere to marry two people.'

'I must go back,' he said suddenly, knitting his brows. 'I cannot stay here any longer.'

'You intend to leave me on my own here?'

'Don't worry,' he said. 'I promise everything will be all right. We will sort things out one at a time. I must go. If I don't, I'll lose my job, in which case, how will I be able to afford to pay for your and Danial's costs?'

The fear of losing him had already taken over my soul - a dreadful affliction mingled with the fear of being dependent on someone I had become so used to. I noticed his restlessness until he declared out of the blue that he had to go back to Stockholm that night to look after his daughters the following day. The shock of that news was so overwhelming and painful that it took a while before it sank in. I'd been living with the delusion that he would be unable to live without me for even a day. He appeared embarrassed at the time of departing. He hugged Danial, promising he would bring him many Legos when he returned.

'Look after yourself and Danial,' he said, hugging me tightly. 'I'll see you soon.'

I didn't know how to stay here without him. Before meeting Johan, I was another woman who had lived in this godforsaken place. However, I had discovered a different aspect of my life after being with him, and I was no longer that wretched woman. He had entrapped me.

'Good that he left, you foolish girl,' Goli said after hearing about his departure. 'Your self-deception has come home to roost. How could you trust him? After spending two summer months of his holiday beside you, he had his fill of sex with you and buggered off.' She added with a snigger: 'Listen to me, you thickhead. These Swedish men don't give a toss about such things as love and all that crap. You think as if he were a bloody eighteen-year-old. You do realise that we're talking here about a man of forty-four years old!'

Danial was the only one who understood me better than anyone else. He could easily sense whenever I was sad or hurt. He had a good understanding of my emotional upheavals that worried me. He always reacted to my crying by putting on a long face.

'Why are you crying, Mummy?' he would sometimes ask.

Johan had carried me high up to the summit of the mountain and let me fall to the bottom of the valley. My body ached, like when you dream of being pushed from the top of something high.

I was ignoring not only my son but also everything around me. I was feeling like a complete idiot. I kept saying to myself: 'You're a fool. Didn't you see that he was amusing himself with you?'

'You must sort out your affairs in the American Embassy,' my mother said.

But I didn't want an invitation letter to obtain an American visa. It was nothing but balls to me. I was sick and tired of everything. What was this absurd and cruel game that life was playing on our lives precisely when our dreams were about to come true? I had been hoping to go to America for a long time, but I wanted to be with him now.

Hoping he would call, I stayed at home for the whole week. But he didn't ring. A dreadful feeling of disquiet that he might have been lying about seeing his children had started to gnaw into my soul. How could he not even call or send me a text? Counting the seconds and minutes hoping to hear from him, mingled with a killing pain, had almost crippled me. How can one love someone like this? How can we find out how life-weary someone has become after wandering wretchedly in the winding alleyways of life by just looking at her fingertips or listening to her heartbeat?

Goli came to see me at the weekend and helped me to arrange an interview on the 14th of November at the American Embassy.

'Go to America, forget all about him, and think that you'd never met him,' she said. 'How lucky you are that you're going to the Promised Land where people are all equal without discrimination – black-skinned, yellow-skinned, red-skinned, Caucasians, white and red geese are all equal! I've heard that in America, the first thing they ask you is where you come from, and you can proudly tell them about your origins and even ask them where they come from. All the people here hope to go to America one day, and you want to go there too, where you'll have everything and live a comfortable life.'

Talking to Goli had made me so depressed and hopeless that I thought everything had ended. I felt very low, and she was my only good friend, a friend with her Iranian peculiarity.

'You know, Goli,' I said. 'He has stolen my heart. I can't help it.'

Not hearing from Johan for a while, I was beset with worrying questions about where he was. Had he met another woman during his nightly wanderings from bar to bar, taken her home, and was whispering in her ears? I was sure he would call me and would come back to me. But I didn't hear from him. Waiting all the time for him to contact me, I went through a difficult time. He neither phoned nor even sent a simple text message. The last message I had from him was: 'I miss you already my Iranian princess!'

I picked up the phone a thousand times to call him, but I couldn't bring myself to do it. More than anything else, I was angry for not knowing what might happen next. Strangely enough, he seemed to me to be increasingly close and aloof. I kept asking myself, where could he go and find anyone better than me? Finally, being angry deep inside and feeling completely let down and wretched, I decided to put him out of my mind. Soon I began to imagine that he was treating me like an idiot.

Imagining all sorts of things in this manner, two weeks passed until the day he called me. Then, after a long silence that made me think that the call might have been cut off, I heard him say: 'When can you come to Stockholm?'

8

I dreamed of holding her body in my arms and
embracing the human being inside her.

Marcel Proust

No sooner had we arrived at the north platform than
the bus stopped. I grabbed Danial's hand and went to
the Pendeltåg train station. The coaches were packed
with people. A middle-aged man made some space for
Danial to sit down. It was hot inside the coach. A man
was reading his paper while most passengers were
fiddling with their mobiles, and others were listening to
music. I looked out of the window—the houses with
terracotta tiles, different types of buildings, trees, and
occasionally people all passed by. Goli was supposed to
come to T-Central to take Danial with her.

While waiting for Goli, we went up to Åhléns
department store on the first floor. I tried on a few
blouses and chose the one I thought was the most
beautiful I had ever worn. Then, reaching down to the

top of my knees, I saw a blue blouse with black lace cuffs fringed with the same lace around its middle. I thought how delighted Johan would be when he saw me in that blouse. My suntanned skin blended beautifully with the colour of the blouse. I kept it looking so good in it, and the sales assistant removed the alarm and paid for it. Then, I went to the cosmetics department on the ground floor, applied deep blue eyeshadow to my eyelids, put more lipstick on, and sprayed Lancôme cologne on my neck. Drumming and trumpeting, a band of musicians in blue uniforms decorated with yellow galloons marched through Sergel Square. The band had gone when I came out of the store, but I could still hear them.

'What have you done to yourself?' Goli said, looking me up and down. 'He'll faint if he sees you like this, girl!'

Seeing me, Danial grabbed my knees. I tried to push him away gently, but he held on tightly to my knees again. Finally, Goli bent down and said to him quietly: 'Say bye-bye to your mummy now.'

Danial's large eyes were filled with tears. I could not understand how a child, who was so restless, could feel. No, this was not part of my plans. I had to leave him at once to prevent myself from becoming more worried. Goli promised she would buy Danial a burger from McDonald's and then go to the park together. She asked me to promise her not to go to Johan's house that night because there was no bus service to the village during the holidays. Besides, I was supposed to spend time with Goli that weekend.

Throughout the two weeks since Johan left, I searched for his name on Google. His name was on many websites, management programmes, seminars, and essential individuals. I had found so many links that had something to do with his business affairs and activities that didn't make sense to me. I also found where he lived, his salary, and how many square metres his house was. Using Google Maps I had also been able to see his house and its windows from above. His house was somewhere in the network of narrow streets in Gamla Stan – the oldest part of the city. I had only passed through it a few times. The houses there had kept their traditional style. At the corners of steeply sloping streets boutiques or cafés could be seen. With polished bricks and wooden doors the houses there reminded one of the old folks of this land who, despite being old and frail, still stood upright on their feet. The clacking of my high heels was echoing on the cobbled street. I felt as though I had seen this scene several times in my dreams.

I kept repeating to myself the Swedish sentences I had memorised. I had a bone to pick with him by telling him he had no right to bugger off and ignore me like that.

I walked towards the Nobel museum and arrived at a square with a statue in the middle. The gurgling of the water could be heard from the fountains around a pool in the middle of the square. Johan was standing beside an old café. My heart was beating like an infant's. I forgot everything I had prepared to tell him when he held me in his arms and kissed me.

He had booked one of the most expensive restaurants in Strandvägen, where the small cruise ships docked along the pier. When in the restaurant, I felt I was a different person. Peculiarly eyeing us, people were looking at his chic suit, polished leather shoes, and silk handkerchief in his suit pocket.

Facing one another, we sat at a table. For a few minutes, neither of us spoke

'I missed you!' I said, gazing into his eyes.

'What I was searching for in his eyes was love. Instead, he was looking at the menu handed over to him by the waiter.

'Can I order something for you?' he asked.

I nodded affirmatively. He asked the waitress to pour some white wine into the long-stemmed glass on the table. He then asked me to taste the wine which I did. Seeing that I liked it, he nodded to the waitress that it was okay. Next, he ordered me steak, chips, fish, and white sauce.

'I prefer red wine,' I said in a low voice.

'White wine goes with fish,' he reminded me quietly.

'Oh God, how long ago is it since I went to a posh restaurant?' I said, pressing my lips together. Then, munching his salad, he just looked at me.

'Why don't you say something?' I went on. 'Where have you been? Why did you keep so quiet? Didn't you miss me?' He remained silent. I could hear his breathing.

'What are you playing at by being so quiet?' I repeated.

'I'm so sorry,' he said finally. 'I don't love you anymore.'

Upon hearing this, I choked on the wine. He stood up quickly, tapping my back and kissing my hair.

'I love you, you silly girl,' he said. 'Do you get it?'

'I quickly left the table and went to the toilet downstairs. I was still coughing when he walked into the toilet, grabbed my hips from behind, and said: 'I love your sexy hips.'

He would always do things at the right time that made me happy. Acting like a classy woman in front of the mirror, I curled my hair behind my ears, washed my hands, and examined my teeth. Then, looking severe, I brushed imaginary fluff off my blouse with my fingers. I was pretty satisfied with myself, particularly when my eyes became dreamy after a glass of wine. I felt the air I was breathing was full of his scent. All I was thinking about was being with him. I wanted him with an overpowering desire. He was standing in the men's section, splashing handfuls of water on his face. He raised his head no sooner than I grabbed his neck from behind and bit his earlobe, making him utter loudly, 'Hey!'

'Let's go and have our coffee somewhere else,' I said.

National anthems were being played in some shops. The middle-aged women with heavy make-up, garbed in yellow-and-blue traditional costumes, paraded in the square, looking like invading conquerors. A fresh breeze was blowing in from the sea, and the seagulls glided high above. The bright daylight flooded the buildings, the trees, the cafés, the cobblestones, and the people.

It was as though I was seeing the people, the cafés, the lanes, and the street corners from a new angle. Wherever I went with him, I saw *his* face no matter who was around us.

'Why are you looking at me like that?' I asked him.

'You look around, and I look at you,' he said.

Seeing that a man was eyeing me, Johan looked at me and said with a scowl: 'Does he know you?'

'No. Why should he know me?' I answered.

'You know what?'

'What?'

'A lot of people are jealous of me.'

'Why is that?'

'Because I have you.'

That was the reassurance I was waiting for. He walked into an expresso café on Drottninggatan Street. He ordered a double cappuccino for me without asking what I wanted. We sat at a table near the window. Licking her ice-cream, a little girl with her face painted like a rabbit was staring at us.

'A story has been going around about this street,' he said, pointing outside. 'Every year, the ghost of a girl wanders out of that opposite castle and takes away someone with her.'

'Every street and lane has a story to tell,' I said. 'Sooner or later, we two will be stories that happened in this street, isn't that so? I also know the story of a woman dressed completely in red, who would appear every day for many years exactly at four o'clock in Ferdowsi Square in Tehran. She would then go round and round the square, looking around to see if her man would show up. Having jilted her, the man never came to the rendezvous. Wearing the same red dress and red lipstick, the wretched woman did this even long after the Revolution.'

'Had you seen her at all?' Johan asked.

'Not personally,' I answered. 'But many people had.'

'So, what happened to her then?' he asked. 'Did her man come back or not?'

'I don't know,' I said. 'No one knew what happened to her. During the Revolution, the street urchins pelted her with stones because she was not wearing a hijab. Some women gave her presents as tokens of vows they had made.'

'Vows for what?'

'They did that to have good luck in their romantic relationships,' I explained. 'Rather like what lovers do here in Europe. For example, when they toss coins into that fountain in Rome to find the love of their lives or when folks in London jump into the pools in Trafalgar Square on Christmas Day.'

'It's absurd, isn't it?'

'Yes,' I agreed. 'Everything she wore was red – her clothes, watch, handbag, and even shoes. She looked like that Red Queen in Lewis Carroll's *Through the Looking-Glass, and What Alice Found There*.'

'You mean the queen who was constantly on the move?'

'No, that was the Queen of Hearts in *Adventure of Alice in Wonderland*,' I corrected him. 'Do you know what the Queen of Hearts' answer to Alice's question, 'Why do you keep moving?' was?'

'No, I don't.'

'The Queen of Hearts replied to Alice, 'My dear, here we must run as fast as we can just to stay in place,' I explained. 'It took the critics many years to discover the hidden message in that statement about the evolutionary process of constantly being on the move, meaning that stagnation means extinction.'

'All that being true, I hope you're not trying to tell me that the Red Queen inspired this woman-in-red in Lewis Carroll's book?'

'I don't see why not,' I said, looking at my watch. 'I must go and pick up Danial now.'

'Where are you off to?' he said. 'I thought you were going to stay with me.'

'No, I there wasn't such a plan.'

'Please,' he said. 'I've missed Danial. Ask Goli to keep Danial tonight. Then, we'll pick him up tomorrow, and we'll all go to the Skansen Museum. Have you ever taken Danial there? I'm sure he'll like it. Children love that place.'

His voice sounded like the night when he kept asking me to go to his grandfather's house.

'Why don't you stay with me over the weekend?' he insisted. 'There's enough space in my flat for you and Danial. Tomorrow he can sleep in my daughters' bedroom.'

There was something in his voice that persuaded me to follow him quickly. He was the kind of man who made me feel more beautiful. I felt as though I had become a woman once again.

There were almost no books on the bookshelves in his flat. There were also no houseplants in his bedroom except a geranium on the table with dead leaves. A hot-water bottle lay on the bed beside a plastic bag full of dirty clothes.

'I left my house, and all I had to my ex-wife,' he said. 'The day I left home, all I took with me was a bag full of my clothes.' He then added: 'Do you accept me as I am?'

Without answering him, I stood on my heels and kissed him. I then took off my blouse and rapidly unbuttoned his shirt. He unbuttoned his cuffs, pulled his shirt down to his arms, and pressed my naked shoulders against him. He pushed me against his muscular belly. Touching his trousers, I clutched his erect penis and made him sigh loudly. I squatted before him, unbuttoned his trousers, and pulled down the zip. I then gently slipped my hand inside his underpants, massaged his penis and all of a sudden inserted it into my mouth. Sucking his penis, I looked up and saw that he had closed his eyes, tilting his head backwards. He thrust his hands into my hair and caressed it. He then gently lifted me up and unhooked my bra. My heart was beating fast and I was on fire. He kept murmuring into my ear: 'Oh God, I love you so much.' He sat me on the bed, dug his face into my hair and kissed my lips hard. He went on kissing my neck and chest until he locked his lips on one of my nipples. He then began licking my belly until he reached down to my underpants which he swiftly pulled off. He licked my labia and gently pushed his fingers into my moist vagina. I was too excited to keep still. He raised his head and told me not to move. Writhing with pleasure I was unable to remain still. I thought I knew that body. Being able to see his blue veins beneath his white skin, I felt as though our bodies had become one by being perfectly united.

The room was filled with the noises and scents of lovemaking. Finally, when I felt coming, I locked my legs around his hips, wanting to have his semen inside me. Instead, he quickly pulled out his penis and ejaculated onto my belly.

That night was another of the best nights I had spent with him. He was not only the man I had let into my body but also my soul, feeling his presence in all of my being. It was as though this was the strongest sentiment I could experience in this troubled and contradictory world that made me feel safe.

It was about dawn that I had a strange dream in which Sina held Danial's hand. All three of us were walking on a wooden bridge. I watched the water's powerful current in a deep ravine under the bridge. I could hear large pebbles mingling with someone's warm breaths. Looking around, I saw Johan, who didn't look like his usual self. Holding Danial's hand, he was running away. The bridge was shaking roughly. As I ran after them, the bridge gave way, and I was thrown off...

Probably hearing me crying, Johan had woken and was saying to me: 'Shush, shush. You had a bad dream.' Then, seeing me still crying, he put his hand around my waist. Then, finally, he got up and brought me a glass of water.

'Promise you'll never leave me alone!' I begged him. 'I have no one else here except you.' For a long while, he gazed at me in silence.

'I was dreaming of my brother, Sina...,' I mumbled.

Casting a glance at him, for an instant, I thought I saw Sina, who was sitting beside me and staring at me.

'When you have only one brother, and he is the first one who has introduced you to the outside world,' I explained, 'with whom you've had your first adventures, such as going to the movies, listening to music, and with whom you've spent good times outside the house, and you hear one day he has gone somewhere faraway for good, you feel he has taken part of you with him. You realise that part of your existence has vanished.'

'I cannot imagine how hard that is,' Johan said.

'My brother went to America without telling me,' I continued. 'When I found out, I fell ill with fever and shakes. When I recovered, a sense of rage and hatred replaced my feeling of loss. Despite all this, I kept hoping that he would come back. That's why I don't like waiting.'

'You see, Johan, I'm scared,' I said after facing him and looking into his eyes. 'Promise you'll never abandon me. All my life, I had always been alone, waiting for someone. Finally, that someone happened to be you, sitting here beside me. I can't bear seeing you go, also. I can't endure waiting for you anymore. I'm no longer able to wait for anything.' I could not help sniffling.

'I like it when you sniffle like a little girl,' he said, gently pinching the tip of my nose. He then mimicked me.

'Don't be silly,' I sniffled.

'What are you worried about, darling?' he said. 'Why have you become so upset? Nothing will ever come between us.' He gently stroked my hair and added with a sigh: 'My Eastern miracle, you'll always belong to me. You must forever be mine.'

'Yours?' I repeated, utterly gobsmacked. 'Do you have such things in Sweden? As far as I know, you cannot possess anyone here.'

'Yes, we have,' he said. 'Our love has nothing to do with where we live on this earth. How about a glass of wine?'

'Good idea.'

He got up, put on his underpants, walked to the kitchen, returned with two glasses of wine, and sat on the bed.

'Would you like to hear the rest of the story?'

'My pleasure, my sad princess,' he said, sipping his wine. Then, after a short pause, he asked, 'Did Sina return to Iran?'

'No. He never came back,' I answered. 'One night, he went scuba-diving on a California beach and never came out of the water. The circumstances of his death are unclear; no one ever found out what had gone on before and after his death. His corpse was never returned to Iran. It was not easy to ask for the autopsy results, the coroner's report, and the necessary documents to send the corpse to another country at the other end of the world. There were many rumours about the circumstances of Sina's death, but all of them were just guesswork. My uncle said the forensic evidence showed that Sina had committed suicide. They may have been right, but my father never accepted that Sina killed himself. The truth was that he was dead, and that was, and no one dared question the details of his death. After his death, the removal of his furniture was handed over to a house clearance company. My uncle gave the furniture to charity and kept Sina's belongings in his house. The house that was still there was soon rented, and the money was sent each month to my father. It is close to the ocean where Sina loved to be.' I stopped momentarily, thinking about Sina's house, imagining its details.

'When I go to America, I'm supposed to stay there,' I said, coming back to my senses. 'My father says the house will one day be Danial's. Never taking off his black mourning clothes, my father didn't arrange a funeral ceremony for Sina. No matter how much my mother insisted that they should go to America and live near their son's grave, my father didn't accept. He would tell her one cannot take one's homeland with him wherever he goes. Over the years, my father had grown fond of the courtyard of our house, where you could find so many different flowers, such as dog roses and a variety of roses, snapdragons, and geraniums. He would spend all the spring and summer afternoons in the courtyard watering the flowers. Unfortunately, everything in the house went to rack and ruin after

Sina's death. Neglected by everyone, the flowers withered and died, making one question if once the courtyard was ever alive with flowerbeds and flowerpots.

Johan drained his glass of wine, filled it again, glanced at the time on his mobile, and gently stroked my hair.

'How come you got married?' he asked.

'I don't know,' I said. 'I was hoping perhaps by doing that; I could escape the sad atmosphere in my parents' house. But, unfortunately, after Sina's death, some dreadful melancholy began to reign in our house. I have not been able to rid myself of that painful experience ever since. My father never went back to his everyday life. The strange thing was that he never shed a tear for his son's death. All day long, he would do nothing but watch television. What was he thinking about? Did he think about Sina? One could never tell. He was perhaps thinking about his past life in a country that had brought him to the past he was in.'

'They say our emotions fade as time passes, but that hasn't happened to me. I considered my brother dead to me from the day he left. That's why I was sadder for my parents when I heard the news of his death than Sina's death. One can never lose someone several times. The sadness after losing a dear one is unbearable just after they're gone. I can feel a sinking sense of dread and foreboding that I will lose you too. The fear of losing you has begun to prey on my mind. I don't know how I will go without you.'

'Without me?' Johan said, pointing at his chest. 'No way will I do that unless you want it yourself.'

Suddenly, he dug his face into my hair, kissed my neck, bit my breasts, stuck his tongue into my mouth, and began to smell me as he slid his head down my belly. He then said: 'Do you know what you taste of? Of sweet and sour and candy.' He traced his finger on my belly and said: 'Do you know how many speckles there are on your body? With my eyes closed, I can tell you how many and where they are. Your speckles look like constellations, like astrological figures connecting you and me. I love the way you breathe with all of your body. I love the way you move.'

He held me tight and went back to sleep again. It was past noon when I woke up. His hands were still around me. 'Oh, my God, Danial!' I said out loud.

I had to go and fetch him. Johan asked me to take a leave of absence with no no-pay for the following week. I told him I would email my employers first thing on Monday. It was Saturday, and we took Danial to Skene.

On Sunday, he took me to the Enko Store. He bought me a Phillips designer dress with a simple Swedish style, a leather pair of Swedish Tiger shoes, and boots with fur-lined insides. I thought I had become Julia Roberts in the movie *Pretty Woman*. Carrying all those shopping bags, I became very excited. He had bought many things for me – shampoo, hair-softening spray, body lotion, a sleeping gown, and all I needed. He put a large box in his bedroom for me. He placed my toothbrush, toothpaste, personal things, and Danial's in his bathroom cabinet. Afterward, we went to the Ghent shop and bought a bedspread, a sheet, and towels.

I asked him to let me pay for everything myself as I had enough money. He shook his head and said: 'I know you have money, but these are gifts, darling!' Then, I remembered what my grandmother used to say: 'One man can raise a woman to the skies, and another can trample all over you.' I would laugh thinking of what those older adults used to say!

During the ten days I spent with him, I'd concluded that real love and companionship couldn't be better than that. So I would throw my socks and bra on the sofa, where we lounged beside each other every night and watched television. One attraction of being in such a relationship was that I became excited by merely watching his wrist, his shoulders, his muscular legs when he wore short trousers, and even his bald patch. Looking at his stubble in the mornings, I believe ours was the best type of togetherness. I loved him as one loves an old wine and wouldn't dare drink it if one couldn't cope with all that joy and die.

I had, at long last, succeeded in entering a world far removed from my world. Knowing that my future would be with Johan, I walked steadily on the ground that was now firmly under my feet.

'Danial must go to the best university,' he would say. 'I'll treat him the same way I treat my daughters.'

One day as I was washing Danial's hair in the bath and Johan was cooking the meat and vegetables, my mobile rang. He handed me the mobile. It was my mother on a video call. She already knew I was with Johan. When I started talking to my mother, he stood behind me and said: *'Salaam, khoobi. Khodaa haafez!'*

'He sounds very sweet when he speaks Persian, doesn't he?' I said, laughing aloud.

Danial joined me with his towel and watched my mother's distorted face on the mobile screen. No sooner had she seen Danial than she said: 'Oh, my sweetheart... my baby!' She then asked me: 'How are you getting on?'

'I'm good, very good!' I answered, closing my eyes and taking a deep breath. 'Danial's good too.'

'What would you like a granny to buy you for your birthday?' she asked, looking at Danial. Baffled, Danial looked at me.

'My sugarplum,' she went on asking: 'What would you like me to send to you?'

'I...,' Danial said after thinking a bit.

'Is that mankind to you, my love?' my mother cut him short.

She kept bombarding my son with questions. Finally, I snatched the mobile from Danial and said: 'I don't think it's a good idea to worm answers out of a child, Mother.'

'Good idea?' my mother snapped. 'What do you know about what's good and bad?' She then asked sharply: 'When will you come back home?'

'I'll be back soon,' I replied.

There followed one of her feigned pauses.

'What do you mean by that?' she asked finally. 'What'll happen to Danial?'

'Please, mother,' I said. 'Don't start the same argument again.'

'What argument?' she went on. 'This is not the first time you won't listen to us. So I'm asking you if you realise what you're doing. Have you sorted out your affairs with the American Embassy? You know that the date of your invitation to go to America will soon end?'

'Yes, I know.'

'I don't think it was a good idea to move in with that man,' she said. 'You should've given it some more time to get to know him better.'

'Please, Mother!' I said. 'I want to do what *I* like for a while. Everything is all right. We go on trips with Johan. Everything is fine. Danial is thrilled.'

She let out a heavy sigh and fell silent.

'Aren't you happy for us, Mother?' I asked.

'Suit yourself,' she broke her silence in a resigned tone of voice. 'You've never listened to us. You can do whatever you like; only remember you can't afford to be reckless this time. All you have to do is to think of that unfortunate child. A little boy always needs a father, do you understand?'

I was just about to say it was none of anybody's business and that what I was doing was entirely rational. But, I held my tongue because that was precisely what I had said to my parents when I was marrying Isaac. So I just bit my lower lip and kept quiet.

Without saying goodbye, my mother hung up. I didn't expect her to talk to me in such a sharp tone. After I put my mobile down, Johan came up and asked: 'What's the matter? Your lip is bleeding.'

He wiped the blood with tissue paper. I didn't know what to tell him. 'My mother is worried,' I just said.

'Would you like to go out?' he asked.

'Is Danial coming with us?'

'No. Maybe Goli could look after Danial tonight.'

I had to convince Goli to look after Danial while we were out. Danial looked happy when I helped him out of the car to hand him over to her. He stretched out his hands, kissed me hard as children do, and went with her.

John and I went to a cinema and watched a melodramatic movie. When we came out again, I saw small groups of drunken passers-by aimlessly wandering in no particular direction. Trooping into different bars, they listened to either famous Swedish or American music of the eighties.

Dressed up in a shiny get-up like a woman, a man with heavy makeup kept staring at me in such a way that I was reminded that I was still a foreigner.

'I envy you,' I said to Johan in a low voice, unconsciously putting my arms around him. 'You belong to such a beautiful city like Stockholm. Here you have it all – civilisation, a highly developed country, intermingled traditional buildings with nature, and virgin nature all around.'

The people around us were making so much noise at that hour of the night that they wouldn't hear us speak. 'But your beauty makes me jealous,' he said in a low voice to my ear, despite the racket around us. 'No. Here is your homeland too.' I shook my head, letting him know that it wasn't. 'I guess it's time you accepted that you belong to this city and country too.'

'It can only be a homeland for me as long as I'm with you,' I said. 'Being with you makes me forget the pain of exile.'

'I'm so pleased to hear that you no longer feel you are an exile here,' he said after kissing me.

***

We were now in the middle of autumn, and we had only seen one another at weekends. I was so preoccupied with work Danial had started going to nursery, and I didn't notice how the weekdays came and went. I thought Johan would love me more when I had a job.

'You must become part of this society,' he kept reminding me.

I was prepared to do any job to show him I belonged to this country by paying my taxes.

I would try to find all sorts of excuses to go and see him, but he would always say he had to work all day and that I would find it difficult to live with.

'It wouldn't be fair on you to come to the city only to go back at two o'clock to pick up Danial,' he would say.

'No, that's not fair. Wait until next week after my daughters leave.'

Having waited for him the whole week when he was supposed to come to see us, he sent a text with a kiss on Friday night saying that he wouldn't be able to go because his daughters had decided to stay over the weekend.

I phoned Johan, who politely apologised, causing me to lose my temper.

'Why did you promise that you'd come?' I asked him. 'Why don't you come with your daughters? It's about time you introduced them to me!'

'No, not yet,' he replied. 'They're not ready for this. They may need more time. But I promise I'll come next week.'

'No need to do that,' I blurted out. 'After your children leave on Sunday, you could take a few days' leaves and come and see me!'

I heard banging sounds in the corridor as though someone was hammering a nail into the door. It was Danial who was knocking his toys on the wall. I motioned to him to keep quiet. Instead, he kept banging even louder.

'I'm thirsty, Mummy,' he shouted.

'Go and see what Danial wants,' Johan said.

'Just a minute,' I said. 'When are you coming here?'

'I can't,' he answered. 'You don't want me to lose my job, do you?'

'In that case, I'll come and see you,' I said. 'I'll ask Goli to look after Danial.'

'No, she cannot always look after your child.'

'Don't you worry about her,' I said. 'I'll arrange with her.'

'No, that's not possible,' he said. 'You must go to your work.'

Feeling upset after a disappointing exchange, I hung up, poured all the wine left from the night before into the glass, and drank it in one go.

On Saturday, Goli came to see me.

It's time you finished with him,' she advised me. 'He's playing games with you.' Feeling deeply anxious, I tried to go over what had happened so far without coming to any conclusion. Not willing to go to any decision, I thought I was tormenting myself by living with ambiguity mingled with false hope.

Nothing is more boring than faithfulness,' Goli said. 'What's the use? My poor mother was faithful to my dad all her life, nursing him throughout the years he became bedridden with cancer. Guess what happened after he died? We found out that he had a son from another wife! How is such a thing possible? This teenage son showed up at his funeral and washed my father's grave. Would you believe it? Interestingly, my mother, who was not prepared to believe it, kept saying: 'These are all nothing but lies. Your father was the most decent man....' I don't trust anyone. Why can't we be just like men?'

As the days came and went, I thought I was losing my mind. Johan had to work when his daughters were not with him during the week. If it wasn't for Danial, I could see him. Not having shown up at the weekend, I put Danial's iPad with its charger and his toys in a bag and extra clothes for myself in mine, and we went to Stockholm. In a squalid-looking hairdresser, I had my hair coloured blond. I looked somewhat off-putting with blond hair and brown skin, but I thought he might like my new look. Danial and I went to his house. He had just come back from work.

'No. That's not a good idea,' he said, looking shocked.

'What's not a good idea?' I asked. 'My coming here.'

'No, darling. I mean your hair.'

'I thought you liked blond women.'

'It's lovely,' he said, raising his eyebrows. 'But I prefer you with your brown hair.'

Sitting in front of his computer, he glued his eyes to the screen. Then, not paying any attention to what he was doing, I stood beside him and plonked the documents I had to email to the American Embassy on the table, asking him: 'Can you scan these and email them to me?'

'What are these?' he said, frowning.

'Documents for the American Embassy.'

'What for?'

'To apply for a visa, of course.'

'Whose visa?'

'In two weeks, I'll have an interview for my visa application on the 14th of November that I had forgotten to tell you about.'

He got up, put his glass of wine on the cabinet, filled it up, knocked it back, and said: 'What are you doing this for?'

'Well, I must go to America!'

'Tell me you don't wish to abandon me,' he shouted suddenly. 'Go on, tell me.'

'I don't know,' I said. 'Maybe I'm doing it for Danial.'

His nervous reaction caught me off guard a little. Looking sideways at us, Danial appeared to have become frozen with fear.

'So, this is it. You deserve the best,' he went on. 'Any man dreams of being with you. I'm not good enough for you.'

'No, don't say that,' I said.

'That's right, America,' he said, tone aggressive after tossing off a second glass of wine as swiftly as the first one.

'What do you mean by that?' I asked. 'The thing is that I, I....'

Before I could finish my sentence, he quickly picked up his tracksuit and left the flat, shutting the door behind him. The water in the pan had started to boil, letting out steam. I poured just enough pasta into the pan for Danial, rinsed Johan's wineglass, and placed it in the dishwasher. What had I done to make him behave like that?

When he came back, he was quiet. After taking a shower, he came and lay beside me. Without kissing or touching me, he took off my clothes. His head and face were soaked with sweat. Squeezing my breasts very hard, he bit one of my nipples. He thrust his penis so hard inside me as though he wanted to cleave my body into two halves. Screaming, I briskly turned over, fell on my back, and tried to push him away. But he started from behind. Trying to make him back again, he pulled my hair. As I screamed involuntarily, he put his hand on my mouth.

He was groaning repulsively. Finally, he let go of me, and I lay there lifelessly. In the morning, I found myself lying in bed like a corpse. I touched the blood-stained sheet. All my orifices were sore. Not knowing what had happened to me, I struggled to my feet and took a shower.

Once all three of us sat in the car, he glanced at Danial to make sure he had fastened his seatbelt. After securing his seatbelt, he reversed the car without even looking at me. Throughout the whole journey, he seemed very edgy. I was surprised to see him treating me like a stranger. With his face so grotesque, he only took us to Stockholm's central station instead of to Uppsala, where he was supposed to take us.

'Why did you stop here?' I asked him when he stopped the car.

'I can't go any further as I'll be fined,' he grumbled.

Without getting out of the car to kiss me goodbye, he waited for me to help Danial out of the vehicle.

Struck dumb, I stood there in the pouring rain. It was as though the dome of heaven had been cracked, letting rainwater down in torrents.

'It's all over,' I said to myself. 'No way will I talk to him again.'

For a moment, I thought of deleting his number. But I had no willpower to do that.

The bleeding never stopped the whole week. So he didn't come at the weekend.

'I had told you that my priorities are my daughters,' he succinctly explained when I wanted to know why. 'They've just come back here. Nothing is more important for a Swedish father than his children!'

I don't know why I hadn't noticed he wanted to dump me!

9

You robbed me of three things:
My patience,
My sanity,
My sleep.
Rumi (Persian poet, 1207-1273)

On Monday morning, I took Danial to the nursery.
It was ten o'clock when I arrived in the city. I thought it
would be a good idea to go to his workplace and talk to
him over lunch. I badly wanted to see him. But how
could I do that after not talking to him for more than
ten days? I couldn't bear not being close to him. So I
told him in a text message that I had come to Stockholm
and was waiting for him. As he didn't answer, I thought
he either hadn't looked at his mobile or perhaps he was
in a meeting and would answer once the meeting was
finished. So I wandered around the Ericsson Globe. I
bought a pair of shorts and a purple bra with pink
flowers on sale in the Lindex Store. After I checked my
mobile, I saw that he had read the message without
answering. As I was thirsty, I bought a coffee that smelt
of piss.

The chilly wind was too blustery for the birds with feeble wings to fly in the sky. So I called the nursery and told them I would be there at five o'clock. I was told Danial wasn't feeling well and was coughing a little, and this caused me to become worried and anxious about him. But I was unable to forget about Johan either. I had to see him.

I called him on his work mobile number. It was past noon. After waiting a long time, I texted him again, begging him to answer my call as I had something important to talk to him about. He called back after a short time.

'Why don't you answer my messages, you idiot?' I shouted into the phone, not letting him say anything. 'I've been waiting outside your office. It's now three o'clock. Don't you even have a minute to come down and see me?'

'We were not supposed to meet, were we?' he said after a long pause.

'But...,' I muttered.

'I can't see you, honestly,' he replied. 'I think it's better not to talk now. I don't want us to argue.'

I did my best to keep my composure.

'How can you treat me like this?' I implored him after quickly changing my tone. 'Why are you trying to hurt me? Please come down so I can see you just for one minute!'

'I'm sorry; I don't want to upset you,' he said. 'But I can't see you. At least not now. I think that will make the situation much worse.'

I found his unfeeling cold voice shocking.

'This is not right for either of us,' he exclaimed after hearing my sniffling over the phone.

He hung up on me before I could say anything. I was feeling feverish and cold. I took the metro to the city's central station. Coming out of the metro, I found the ever-thickening fog had cloaked the upper parts of the trees.

Mysterious-looking shadows lurked everywhere in and out of the fog. With every step I took, I imagined I had come to some end, and after turning every corner, I thought I had come to the end of the world. Everywhere looked like an alien world to me. I thought I was lost. I looked at the time on my mobile. The nursery would close in five minutes. I walked as fast as I could and even run. But it was no use. I had missed the bus that would take me to where we lived. It would be costly if I were to take a taxi. So I waited for the next bus to our town to come and then planned to take a taxi.

I felt colder and colder by the minute. The darkness brought with it more heavy rain, and the streets started to glisten under the pale streetlamps. I was at a loss as to what to do. I had no more courage left in me to think of anything – where Danial was, or why was there no answer to Eric and his wife's phone?

I wish I had stayed in Iran. I now felt the pain of exile more than ever. Why did I come here where I had no one? Why did I nurture the notion that if I changed my homeland for the present one, I could also change myself? I wish I had supported Isaac! I wish I hadn't left him alone. Why didn't I weep after he died? We might have had a good life together. Self-doubts had already begun to gnaw into my soul. I was sick of everything here – its cold and smug people, its clockwork law system, and its freezing dark weather. Having become filled with bitterness, I wouldn't say I liked the whole world.

One hot summer day, after the lecture, more than six of us were sitting in a park near the university when a gypsy woman with heavy mascara and wearing a spangled dress approached us.

'Hey you, pretty one, let me take a look at your hand to tell your fortune,' she addressed me after spotting me among the others. 'You don't have to pay me anything!'

'Why don't you tell our fortunes?' said the other girls, laughing.

The gypsy woman clasped my hand in hers. But, first, she examined the lines in my palm and peered into my eyes.

'You'll leave this country,' she said. 'You'll continue your life in a country surrounded by water.'

I became happy hearing this, and I said to my friends: 'She means America.'

'You'll roam around a while just like a wandering Jew,' the gypsy woman went on. 'You'll not belong anywhere in this world. Your destiny is to wander here and there all at sea.'

Whatever that gypsy woman had told me years ago had come true. I took the next bus. I felt nauseous due to so much stress. Why did I leave Iran? Why did everything remain the same? Why didn't I stay put in my homeland? Why did I come here to beg for so many things, whether good or bad? Whatever for? Only because there may be a brighter future for me! I didn't see any hope on the horizon as life was getting harder and harder. Hmm, America! Why the devil should I go there? I must stay here. It would help if you stayed and changed things wherever you were. The world has become a callous place. The age of emigration is over. Even the birds no longer migrate. I remembered a documentary on Iranian television about migratory birds. Half of the birds die before reaching their destination, and the other half are hunted once they settle down in their new home. Damn it! Why is it always either too early or too late to depart?

The passenger beside me got off the bus, and I wept throughout the journey. I was missing the homeland that I loved, where I could see the footprints of my childhood dancing, where I swung hanging from her ancient trees, and where even I had my disturbing dreams in her prison. I loved my homeland, which was very unkind to my generation. Had I stayed, however, had we all survived and resisted, the conditions would have been better for future generations. Why should we change our homeland? We cannot change our history by changing where we live. We must stay put and fight. Nothing is happening anywhere in this world. Stay wherever you are, and grin and bear it! People like me were just like others, only unfortunate to have ended up in a land that was not our homeland.

'No matter what creed you believe in,' my father used to say, 'you have to fulfill your responsibilities towards the land in which you're born!'

I felt more and more scared as I approached the village. Soon after arriving home, I knocked gently on Eric's door. After some minutes that seemed like a century, he opened the door. Then, with his face hidden in the shadows and his eyes glinting in the dark, he looked at me angrily.

'Danial!' I stammered. He stepped aside, letting me in. I hugged Danial, who was asleep on the sofa. I heard Eric's wife bustling in another room. When I lifted Danial, the blanket slipped off through my fingers.

'Take the blanket with you,' Eric said sharply. 'It's raining outside. The child will catch a cold.'

Danial opened his eyes when I put him in bed and lay beside him. I put his sleepy warm face against me. His hair was wet and warm with sweat. I pushed aside locks of hair stuck to his damp forehead and kissed it. I don't know if my tears or his sweating made it so wet.

I turned him over and put the pillow under his head. He wrapped himself in the blanket.

'Do you feel better?' I asked. 'Did granddad Eric pick you up from the nursery?'

'Yes.'

'Are you hungry?'

'No, mummy, I want to sleep.'

'Do you know that Johan is gone now?'

He looked at me with sleepy eyes.

'Will you miss him as I do, my child?' I murmured.

Danial didn't answer. When I glanced at my mobile, there were no messages from Johan. He didn't contact me at all. Counting the seconds and minutes for him to call me had mingled with an unknown fear crippling me.

How could it be possible to love someone like that? Trying to control myself, I didn't call him until the weekend. It was a difficult situation. Then, without warning, he showed up at the weekend. He was wearing a white shirt with a black suit. He looked so handsome that I wanted to hug him despite not being happy with him. As I walked up to him, he took one step backward.

'I must talk to you!' he said.

After coming in, he walked straight into the kitchen, pulled up a chair, and asked me to sit down, saying: 'Sit down a minute!'

When he started talking, he heaved a loud sigh as if trying to stop his tears. He seemed to me a broken man now.

'Don't hate me,' he said finally. 'I did the right thing, do you understand? This way is better for both of us. I'm sorry for everything. I've concluded that we can't continue like this any longer.'

'You're telling me now that it was all a mistake?' I mumbled. 'Now that everything seemed that it was going to be all right?'

He looked as though he was playing the role of someone who had lost everything – a man from whose shoulders hung some heavy weights, rubbing his hands with uncertainty. His playacting seemed farcical.

'We don't have many things in common,' he continued. 'For example, our cultures are very different.'

Those words were all new to me.

'Can you repeat what you just said?' I asked.

'Nothing,' he said. 'I don't want to go on talking too much in case we argue. All is clear, and my staying and talking to you will only spoil our memories together.'

'But why?' I wanted to know.

'Let me finish what I want to say,' he shouted. 'I want to say that I'll never forget you. I want you to remember that.'

'To remember what?'

'The fact that we have had some great times together.'

'You're saying that you want to leave me forever?'

He cast his eyes to the floor to avoid answering my question.

'Please, tell me!'

'Yes, I think this is best for both of us.'

'Go to hell!' I shouted, losing my cool.

'Please!' he said.

'So, that's it then?' I said. 'You want to end it just like that?'

'I don't want us to end up enemies,' he said. 'Just calm down!'

'Why aren't you going then?' I cut him short, having lost my patience.

'Don't talk like that.'

'What are you standing there for?' I went on. 'Why don't you just piss off?'

'I know it's not easy for you,' he said coldly.

'You're a beast. A revolting hyena!' I raved. 'Take a look at your face. It looks like that of a hyena with those sunken eyes and long snout!'

'I didn't want us to come to this,' he said. 'But promise me you'll not hate me!'

'You have no right to tell me this,' I said. 'It is all up to me how to feel about you. You piece of filth!'

'He was sitting in front of me, undecided about whether to leave or stay. I left the kitchen. I tried to calm down. I thought he might follow me. But I heard him closing the door and then starting his car. I couldn't believe he had left. Had he left? I wish I had kept him! I wish I had implored him to change his mind. But how could I do that? He was going through my life as unexpectedly as he had appeared. I had to do something.

I was so stunned and in pain that I felt nauseous. As I was throwing up with my head in the toilet, one thought kept swirling in my head: the vain hope that he would return and apologise. I was confident that he would.

'Mummy... Mummy.' I heard Danial saying.

'What?'

'Are you okay?'

'No.'

He stroked my face, and that made me burst into crying loudly.

'Mummy, I'm scared,' he screamed. 'Don't do that. I'm scared!'

I picked up my mobile and phoned him. He didn't answer. I called him once again. He hung up on me. I sent him this text: 'Please come back, even if for a minute. I've got something to tell you.'

Only one thing was on my mind: he would come back and apologise. However, the last text message I received from him was: 'Don't try to make it worse than it is. I've made up my mind. I'm leaving. This is the right thing to do for both of us.'

Feeling sick, I thought I was going to throw up again. But instead, I knelt beside the toilet basin and vomited. All my muscles had become tense. My chest was achy. My hair was splattered with vomit.

I was sprawling on the toilet floor, looking like I had had an epileptic fit. Danial lifted the lock of hair stuck to my forehead. Droplets of sweat trickled down my cheeks and ended up at the back of my ears.

'Aren't you feeling better now?' Danial asked. 'Get up now, Mummy!'

'No, I can't. I feel horrible,' I moaned.

Feeling sorry for myself, I cried. I had no strength to get to my feet, but I did anyway. I dropped on my back on the bed. Danial stood in the doorway and looked at me as though he was scared.

I heard the banging of the door. I thought it was Johan who had come back. Then I saw Eric standing behind the door, talking to Danial.

'I'm hungry,' Danial said in a quiet voice. 'Eric has made pasta and sausage for me. Can I go?'

Not waiting for my answer, they left, shutting the door behind them. I couldn't remember for how many days I had not eaten. The smell of food made me sick. Danial spent most of his time with Eric and his wife. All I was thinking and caring about was either to have Johan's child in my belly or for him to come back. But it was no use racking my brain to search for reasons for all that had happened. He had gone, and that was that. Yet again, this couldn't be possible. That was the worst thing he could have done to me. Had we not been so attached it would not have been so painful and unbearable for me. I longed for his breath and the smell of his body. He had no right to treat me like that. To hell with that idiot Jean Christophe who had said: 'If we love someone, he has the perfect right to love or not to love us back!'

I was not answering Goli's calls. I hated Eric and his wife's prying eyes. Feeling constantly cold, I kept shivering all the time. I had become fed up with the autumn. Both the days and nights were dark. A demon had started to inhabit my mind. Day by day, I was becoming more and more downcast and worn-out. My mother kept phoning me every day, making me more irritated. To add insult to injury, my father had now joined her, leaving message after message for me. Maybe they were condemned to have begotten me. Everyone in this world was doomed.

'Don't you dare ever leave your son out of your sight,' my mother warned me. 'Why do you let him go to that old man's house? That man might be a pervert and be sexually abusing your child!'

Constantly blaming me, I couldn't go on listening to them. Having no strength to talk, I was scared that I would blurt out my secrets if I spoke to them. Trump had decreed that all Iranian nationals, no matter what religion they believed in, were banned from entering America.

'Come back to Iran,' my mother kept saying. 'What are you staying there for?'

Why didn't they understand that you could never return once you left your homeland? Having become uprooted and turned into outcasts, we are tossed around like dirt and dust by the wind. Nothing mattered to me anymore, nothing. I was finding it difficult to believe that I had now been trapped in this godforsaken village in a freezing country. I was now laughing at that sweet and perfumed dream of America out there beyond the oceans. I had become once again that unwanted, obstinate child that my mother had done her best to stifle in her womb. I was that pig-headed one who wouldn't give in. I wanted to have Johan back, and I didn't know how to go about it.

Very sad and lonely, I was stranded in a remote village with no father, mother, aunties or uncles, no one! But seeing a glimmer of light in the darkness of my life, I still felt hopeful in the face of all that. Like a lonely outcast on a far-off island, I went on hoping against hope. Or I resembled a lunatic, or a condemned convict, or an old, played-out prostitute who goes on living in a vague hope. Hoping that Johan would return, I kept telling myself our relationship would improve. But, not at all being myself, I felt I was now far away from that woman who once had had a taste of happiness. I had become as mournful-looking as my father, as anxiety-ridden as my mother, and as mad as my grandmother. The latter, having broken her hip in a nursing home in California and wheelchair-bound, kept tossing my auntie's jewels out of the window. I had no sense of how the days and nights came and went. This state of affairs went on until the night when Danial started bugging me to read a story to him.

'I can't read to you,' I shouted.

'At least tell me an Iranian story,' he cried.

'Not even an Iranian one,' I yelled at him. 'Go to sleep now!'

'I want milk,' he said, crying louder.

I got a glass of milk for him, which he threw on his bed. I picked up the glass and dashed it against the wall, making shards of glass flow in all directions. I asked him to get up so that I could change the sheet.

His face was flushed. I shook him and pushed him off the bed. All of a sudden, he screamed even louder. A shard of glass had cut his knee. The floor was soon covered with blood. I couldn't go on any longer. Seeing what had happened, I thought I was going mad.

That night he was crying very strangely. I had, of course, seen him crying many times; for example, when he was an infant asking for milk, when he sulked, or just after his birth when the doctor slapped his bottom. But this was a different sort of crying. I lifted him from the floor. Blood was trickling from his knee, and he kept on screaming. I carefully seated him on the chair and started pulling out the pieces of glass one by one from his knee and hands. I wrapped his wounds and changed his clothes. He still kept crying and was very upset; however, I tried to calm him, and he continued.

'You can cry till you die,' I said, leaving the room.

I poured another glass of wine for myself and gulped it down in one go. I did not remember how many drinks I had drunk; I recalled the bottle gets empty. I went outside the cottage and stood beside the door to smoke a cigarette. I saw Eric standing outside. He appeared to have seen everything through the window. He gazed at me as if he had never seen me before. With his messy grey hair, he looked scary. I waved at him. After hesitating, he shouted at me: 'Stupid girl!'

The throbbing in my head was so bad that I dropped onto the bed again. I looked for some painkillers on the small table beside Danial's bed. I couldn't swallow the tablets and couldn't gulp down the water.

I kept retching without throwing up. When I looked at myself in the mirror, I looked like a ghost. Whatever I tried to eat made me feel more nauseous.

Having gone to sleep, Danial had drawn his legs to his belly. He was still and breathed fitfully. Two hours had gone past midnight when all of a sudden, his breathing became rapid and irregular. As if short of breath, he was unable to cough. I dabbed his forehead with a wet handkerchief which soon became warm. I then heard some bizarre noises that sounded like the rattling of tin boxes coming from his throat. His moon-like complexion gradually turned deathly-grey. I placed my hand on his chest. His heart was beating.

I ran out and reached behind Eric's front door. All the lights were out. I drummed hard on the door. No one answered. Shrieking in the yard, I kept throwing stones at his window. I picked up a fistful of pebbles and threw them at the window. Finally, the door was opened.

I don't recall what happened after that. I remember an old clinic with discolored paint on its ceiling, just like the ones you see in Russian films during wartime. A poster showing a young woman with her finger to her lips hung on the wall. It was as though I had lost my power of speech there, as no one could understand what I was trying to say. I was told to keep quiet. When I protested, one of them glared hard at me and, without answering me, walked away as if I were a smuggler or a thief. I felt like a sacrificial sheep that have willingly gone to the slaughterhouse.

I was not able to see Danial. I kept raising my head to see what was going on, but someone stuck an injection into my hand and pushed my head down.

Then I saw Hoshyaar pushing apart my knees hard with his hands, fumbling between my legs. He pulled out a headless baby and handed it over to the woman inspector, who slapped its bottom hard. The formally-dressed man-with-the-pram with a ringless finger, who was standing there, took the headless baby from the woman inspector, held it gently in his arms, and began singing a lullaby to it. After rummaging in the pram, he took out a blanket, carefully wrapped the newborn in it, and without looking around, began to go round the house, whistling as he went. Eric's wife had got out of her wheelchair. She now looked as tall as Alice and ran after Danial outside the house, making faces at me from outside the window. I then heard Eric's laughter getting louder and louder, echoing in the air like the whinnying of a horse. Opening my eyes, I tried to get up. The woman inspector spat on my face, making it wet with spit.

10

I am Nina Tootoonchi, the granddaughter of the Rabbi. I am a seven-year-old pupil with a ponytail tucked under my hijab, sitting on a bench for three in a classroom. I have changed my surname to Nina Baagheri so that I can be accepted into the university to be punched and kicked by the university's Basiji forces. I am Nina Yaghoobzaadeh, in a white wedding gown. The bridegroom is lifting the lace from my face, and everyone starts to holler with joy. I am Veronica with a fake passport in Istanbul on the shores of the cold Mediterranean Sea. I am an exile with no identity in Stockholm, with a bulging belly and hands clutching a little boy's warm hands. I am Nina Peterson, in a wedding gown at Klara Church.

When I came round in, I was in a room. I had a fever. Someone peered down at my face and disappeared. A door was opened, and someone came in. Everything appeared in that shadowy twilight between wakefulness and the unreal land of dreams. I suddenly remembered that Danial had been taken away by the social services, and Johan had gone out of my life for good. They had buried my father without me being at his funeral. I felt as though I was floating in a kind of void. I had heard that only dead fish are carried along with the current. But, hearing every clock tick, I knew I was still alive. I tried to get up, but my head fell on the pillow again.

Then I saw Johan, who was stroking my hair. He then put his head on my chest where he always put it. Feeling my chest becoming heavy, I moved to one side of the bed to make space for him to sit beside me. When I turned my head to look at him, Johan was not there and no one else. Who touched my hair, then? I looked around closely. No one else was in that room except me. I shouted: 'Johan! Danial!' No one answered.

Was it Johan? It could never be him! I soon realised that I wasn't hallucinating. Goli must have told Johan that my father had passed away and that Danial had been taken away from me. I thought he had come to see how I was. I picked up the woolen anorak Johan had bought for me, put it on, and left the clinic in my flowery pyjamas. Everywhere was covered with snow. I ran towards the villa in which I had slept with him for the first time. I saw from a distance that all the window blinds were closed. The tall oak tree, now laden with lumps of snow, stood on the grounds in front of the villa. No one was at home. The only sound I could hear was hammering my hands on the door. But no one opened the door. The door handle was covered with pigeon droppings.

It was as though all was falling into ruins. I walked towards the grocer's opposite the church. My footfalls on the snow made a crunching sound that echoed around. For a moment, I imagined someone was following me. But, looking back, I saw no one. I was wrong.

'The snow looks so lovely, doesn't is,' the grocer said. 'The winters are so beautiful here.'

From how he looked at me, I thought he had never seen such a humiliated-looking person.

'It looks beautiful, just like yourself,' he continued in a melancholy voice. 'The sky looks bright and lovely after the snow, doesn't it?'

The lump in my throat was so big that I found swallowing very hard. Responding to his remarks by nodding, I pulled out my card from the machine. Once outside the shop, I gulped down the hot cup of coffee and lit a cigarette. Everything was buried under the snow – the graveyard, the rubbish heap, everything.

The snow was glistening under the sun, and the ice melted beneath my bare feet as I walked. As I walked, I pulled down the snow-laden branches, and the powdery lumps of snow fell on my face. A handful of stupid pigeons were cooing while mating under the rusty tin roof of the porch of the church. My mobile was disconnected. After I switched it off and then on, there was a message from my father.

'You do realise I'm still your father, don't you?' he said in a feeble voice, devoid of its usual firmness. 'I need to hear Danial's voice or see his face. Pick up the phone. I need to talk to you! I haven't heard that child's voice for a long time.' Then, after a prolonged silence, I heard his fitful breathing, which made my heart beat faster. My mother's grave and harsh voice was the following message: 'Your father left us forever.'

I listened to my father's message more than a hundred times. Why had it all come to this? All I had now in this world was Danial, and I had nothing else to lose. Could there be any affliction worse than this? My grandmother used to say: 'When we face adversity, they first appear out of proportion. But they'll lose their significance as time goes by.' After Johan left me, I wept for my father's death more than anything else. I had to take another path in my life now, a very long one.

I returned once again to my work. I would wake up in the morning, brew my tea, have my pills to calm me down, comb my hair, toss my nightgown on the bed, and have my breakfast, telling myself that all was going well and I was feeling good. Then one day, it dawned on me that I had been deluding myself. I had become exhausted after telling myself all those lies. It had always been like this. Thinking that I was a piece of trash, a helpless refugee with nowhere to go, Johan had easily managed to deceive me and cast me aside. I wasn't that stupid to think that he still loved me and had only left me because he loved me too much. It's not right to hurt and wound someone you love. When you love someone, you want to look after her, care for her, and not hurt her knowingly. I told myself for the last time that it had finished. I didn't even wish to go over his memories. Most of the time, I missed him, but I did my best to go on living. I kept telling myself that it was possible to live a solitary life. I had fallen into the habit of talking to myself. No one paid any attention to me. It was as though I had turned into a phantom. Something was telling me: 'You're now invisible. No one can see you.'

I couldn't afford to be thoughtless and kept asking questions about my situation. What brought me to this pass? The Social Welfare Office had given Danial to a family to look after. According to the reports provided to the Office by his teachers in the nursery, the neighbours, and by judging me by my wretched state of mind, I was deemed not fit enough to care for my son.

What could I do without Danial? I had no motivation whatever. I didn't want to be with anyone except for Danial and Johan.

Day and night, my only contact with other people was to change their nappies and wipe the shit from between their bony legs. I could smell nothing but the smell of older people's excrement. It was as though my only point of contact with people was with the shitty smells coming from below their bellies. I had become used to the foul odours of urine and the smell of medicine. Having become immune to those smells, I had become unaware of the other smells around me. Watching how those older people kept enjoying what was left of their lives by devouring their sandwiches made me feel sick.

I wonder why people go bonkers when they become old. Their mouths water so much for one biscuit that it makes you want to soak all the box of biscuits in their teacups. Whenever I lifted them by putting my arm round their backs, they put all their weight on me as if they were doing it on purpose. Every so often, they mumbled to themselves, making it difficult for me to understand what they were saying. They looked like sad people who were still living in hope, having forgotten that their lives were about to end soon.

Having gone through all those unfortunate experiences, I felt I was treading on water carefully enough so that I wouldn't gulp the water down and drown. It had been a long time since I had not felt pain. But I kept waiting for Johan all the time. I had told him before that I wouldn't say I liked staying. I tried several times to see him but with no success.

I had resigned myself to the fact that he still existed in the most beautiful parts of my dreams, which calmed me down. The problem with the disappearance of your loved ones is that their memories will go to live in your mind. I now didn't care if Johan loved me or not. What mattered was that I was still in love with him. I kept telling myself: 'No, he would never leave me and will stay with me.' I can easily find him in Stockholm. Longing for him, I lived with the delusion of seeing him.

11

Goli and I were lying on the bed beside one another, gazing at the ceiling. It was evening, and we had to go to the disco before ten o'clock; otherwise, we had to pay the entrance fee.

'Oh, my God, we're going to be late!' she jumped up. She then sat in front of the mirror in the corridor.

Goli usually took two to three hours to put make-up on her face. After applying eye shadow, she applied mascara to her eyelashes. The last layer of mascara done, she put on her fake eyelashes. Then she applied some red lipstick which she made look a bit paler by dabbing her lips with tissue paper and putting on a shiny matt lip gloss. Finally, she took a look at herself in the mirror, singing a sad Iranian love ditty that I sang with her:

> *Treading everywhere,*
> *I couldn't find you anywhere.*
> *As I read these pages,*
> *Looking for your image,*

I weep blood for being away from you.
I see your image in brooks and springs.

'Do you reckon we'll see him tonight?' I asked her.

'I think so!' Goli said. 'Take two blankets, go to the McDonald's and get an empty cup, go to his house, sit outside it on one blanket and cover your head with the other, and chant, 'Hello, hello.' Then, as soon he comes out of his house, shows yourself by jumping up and tossing off the blanket. Or even better, why not disguise ourselves in fancy-dress, go to his house, ring his bell, and as soon as he opens the door, you jump on to his neck!'

Slightly annoyed, I cast a glance at Goli. I had never dared tell her that I had, accidentally or intentionally, passed by his house a few times. I was only drawn to his place because I was in low spirits. But I never saw him. I had had my heart in my mouth so many times by seeing someone with a bald patch with a muffler round his neck. Having become like that woman-in-red in Ferdowsi Avenue, I kept going round and round his house in the vain hope of seeing him coming out so that I could catch a glance of him, even if it were only for a minute.

Goli picked up the blusher brush and began to highlight her face. First, she drew a dark line along her nose to make it look more slender and then did her cheeks.

'You deserve it!' she said. 'Having mistreated you, you're still clinging to him. He has been nothing but trouble for you!'

'I nodded as a sign of agreement, pulled my skirt up with difficulty, and backcombed my hair with my hands.

'Take a look at yourself,' she went on. 'Do you realise how many men are dying to be with you, but you're still talking about that arsehole?'

I put on my close-fitting dark blouse, which made my breasts stand out more. Unfortunately, my large breasts were nearly falling out of my blouse, and my hips were about to burst open the seams of my skirt. Then I shook my head a bit. Goli prepared two glasses of hyped-up vodka and gave one to me.

'Cheers,' she said after knocking back her vodka. She then raised her eyebrows, pouted her lips, and said: 'I told you one hundred times don't talk about that arsehole. Don't even think about him!'

When we got on the underground train, we were surrounded by a bunch of men who, according to Goli, wouldn't make an honest man if we put all of them into one.

'Look at them,' Goli said. 'I don't think we can find a nice one among this drunken lot!' She then added: 'How beautiful you look!'

'What do expect with all this make-up?' I said.

We both burst out laughing. We were acting like those upstart women. A few Africans were telling funny jokes to each other and talking loudly. I now believe people talk and laugh louder when communicating in their mother tongue.

We arrived at Östermalm Street. Knowing that Johan was somewhere in the city gave me some hope, making my heart beat faster. I kept seeing his image everywhere. I knew I would see him in one of his hangouts with his friends. It was as though I were waiting for him everywhere and he was the only reason I kept on living. By winning him back, I could once again regain my lost self. Using all sorts of tricks to see him by accident, I wanted him to believe that I bumped into him by pure chance, and only then could we start all over again. I knew that if he saw me one more time, his heart would begin to beat for me. Whenever he saw me in the past, he always used to say: 'I lose my self-control when I see you.'

On Saturday nights, the disco with the music band was held on the first floor of the bar we entered. The music was blaring. Goli walked up to the crowd standing at the bar ordering drinks, bought two glasses of strong beer, found a place, and asked me to sit down. We could see people dancing on the stage from where we were sitting.

Goli took out a lipstick from her handbag, handed it to me, and ordered: 'Go on, put a bit more on!'

The idea that I was not desirable and attractive flashed through my mind instantly. 'Don't just stand there looking mournful,' Goli shouted so I could hear her above the racket. 'You must break the ice by letting yourself go. Turn a blind eye to what your body looks like. Don't fantasise that any minute someone riding on a winged horse will appear and whisk you away! Try to empty your mind. That man you're waiting for will soon come!'

She looked the other way and started talking to some people. I took out my mobile and read Johan's messages all over again.

When I raised my head, I saw an ugly-looking bald man standing before me. I pushed him aside and looked for Goli, but I couldn't find her. Thinking that she might have gone to the toilet or gone outside for a cigarette, I went outside. She was standing beside two men in suits who were smoking. On seeing her, I waved at her. She beckoned me with a smile to join her.

Both men nodded in my direction. One of them eyed me up and down and took a hard drag at his cigar. Goli offered me a cigarette which he lit with his lighter.

'They're proper gentlemen,' she whispered in my ear. 'One of them is a lawyer. Only don't tell them we're Iranians.'

The way we looked showed that we were refugees and didn't belong to the Scandinavian or European race.

'Where do you come from?' the man with a cigar asked us.

'VIP,' Goli answered.

'Could you please tell me where these VIPs come from on this earth?' his friend asked.

'Very Important Persian!' I said, laughing.

An uneasy smile flitted on their lips that meant: 'Why did you escape from that hell to come here?'

'What do you do for a living?' he asked.

'Nothing!'

'Why did you come here then?'

'I don't know.'

'So, you don't know.'

'Don't know what?'

'How many years have you been in Sweden?'

'Three years.'

'Ah, so you're a newcomer!'

I glanced at Goli, who was glaring at him.

'That's right,' I said. 'How do you know?'

'Nothing. I can tell from your accent.'

'Did you know by any chance that if you hear someone speaking another language with an accent, that means she knows one more language than you do?'

'I wonder why Trump has banned Iranians from entering America?' the other man said mockingly in a cold tone. 'What do you reckon?'

'I tell you why,' Goli butted in. 'Primo, all the nations, including your Europe, are made up of immigrants. Iranians belong to the oldest nation from which people haven't emigrated for five thousand years! Secondo, Iran was the first country that established an empire and founded the declaration of human rights. Third, suppose most of us are now driven out of our homeland and have become homeless. In that case, a foreign government has taken control of our destiny. Fourth, most of the Iranian immigrants from Silicon Valley to Wall Street are the best experts in medicine, architecture, and engineering, as well as in many other fields.'

With her neck veins swollen and looking like she was on fire, she kept talking non-stop. The first man, who seemed unwilling to continue with this discussion, threw a sidelong glance at his friend, put his cigarette butt under his foot, and walked off. The other one followed him after saying 'Bye' to us.

I thought how sad and stupid it was that the people of a country could show so much hatred towards the people of another country. All this is because of the idiotic decisions made by our political leaders that make our people suffer under so much pressure. I hated the politicians in the Iranian government more and more for indiscriminately punishing everyone. Goli was right to say that because of our political system, we had been driven out of our homeland and became homeless.

An icy wind began to blow. An older woman was kissing a black-haired teenager.

'Look how these old Swedish women are using the foreigners as sexual slaves,' Goli said. 'The old hags here try to pick up foreign boys, and the old men are after foreign girls. How dare they make fun of us? Didn't I tell you not to tell those guys from what hellhole we have sprung?'

As the tip of my nose had gone numb with a cold, I was not in the mood to go on with any discussion. 'It's freezing out here,' I said to Goli. 'I'm going in.'

The security guard lifted the chain for me to get in. Following me, Goli passed me by and walked straight up to the bar. Raising herself on her heels, she put her face close to the barman's and asked for two more drinks.

Standing stock-still, we drank our drinks. Goli was still fuming. A man walked up to me, grabbed my hand, and took me to the dance floor. He had an athletic body, and he looked all right. Slowly finding our way through the crowd, we ended up on the top floor. Once there, he pulled me towards himself. Moving his body the way he liked, he appeared not to be following the rhythm of the music. Having gone through so much suffering, I felt so rigid that even amid all those warm bodies, my frozen body wouldn't melt.

He kept rubbing his penis against me as he danced. After dancing in the private box, he pushed his lips against mine and thrust his tongue into my mouth so violently that I couldn't breathe. I pushed him off. He then asked: 'Drink?' I nodded affirmatively. He paid for two glasses of vodka with his card. His face was lit up with ecstasy.

'How beautiful you are!' he said.

He knocked back the first drink and then the second one. I could hear the gurgle of vodka in his throat. He guzzled alcohol like someone intent on getting hammered. The florescent lights had made him look pale.

'How about some tequila shots?' Goli said after joining us.

The man motioned at the bar ordering four tequilas. I gulped down the first one in one go and rejected the second one, saying: 'No, thanks.' The man had put his arm tightly around my waist as if he were afraid I might run away from him. He picked up another glass with his free hand and knocked it back.

'You can go with him if you want,' Goli said. 'Only remember, if he oversteps the mark, call the police.'

I followed him out of the bar. As we walked, he stroked my hip.

'Take a taxi!' I told him.

'We can walk,' he said. 'From here to my home, there's only one stop. So what do you say?'

'It's not too far, is it?' I said, taking a deep breath.

'No, it's just behind this Rådmansgatan Street.'

A drunk older man had stripped naked in the cold and raved loudly. He was surrounded by a troupe of drunken and boisterous men and women.

After arriving at where he lived, he opened the main door and entered. I followed him. He switched on the light. The corridor was dark and damp. We reached the door of his flat. When he opened the door, I saw the light on the windowsill lit up some objects in the flat, including a wooden statue of a naked African woman with large gold earrings on the table near the sofa. A cat the size of a bear crept from under the couch and snarled.

On the walls were hung old pictures with discolored and cracked frames. I put my handbag near the door and sat on the sofa without taking off my shoes.

'Whisky or vodka?' he said after aggressively putting his arm around my shoulders.

'Whisky with ice.'

'I like you,' he said after putting the glasses on the table and standing before me.

'So!' I said.

He put on some rock music. 'Do you like this sort of music?' he asked.

'I'm not sure.'

'Take off your clothes!'

'What for?'

'Come on! Pull down your skirt.'

He sat beside me, pushed his hand into my blouse, and squeezed my breasts hard. Then, he drained his whisky in one go and said: 'Knock it back!' I was holding the glass in my hand and twirling the ice cubes stuck together with my finger.

'Oh, how lovely you are!' he said. 'Tell me, what are you after?'

Pausing for a bit, I didn't answer him. The good thing about being with a stranger is that we didn't lie to one another, meaning we could get down to business without beating about the bush.

'Look, I've got a hard-on,' he said after switching off the lamp on the windowsill. 'It's very large. What was your name, by the way?'

Calling to mind my asylum days, I thought of telling him I was called 'Nobody,' just like Ulysses, the king of Ithaca who, after years of exile, had told the monster Calypso that his name was 'Nobody.' But then, I changed my mind on second thoughts, thinking that he might figure I was mad.

'My name is nothing,' I decided to say.

'Really?'

'Yes. What difference does it make?'

'Nothing. I want to fuck you.'

'Yes, I know,' I mumbled. 'Go on, get on with it.'

The earrings of the statue of the African woman soon started to jingle. I lay on the sofa and rested my head on the end of it. Floods of tears flowed from the corners of my eyes and tricked down on to the carpet. I had heard that when people become nude, they resemble each other. But no one's body smelled like Johan's. I would never find anyone like him. No one had the tone of his voice. No one would ever murmur his sweet words into my ear.

At weekends, all we did was frequent bars and nightclubs, sit on the stools, guzzle one drink after another, and have a good time.

Working weekdays, I managed to make ends meet; at the end of each month, I ended up with no cash. So I spent most of my wages on having my nails manicured, on artificial eyelashes, on being tan in a solarium, on hair extensions, on highlighters, on all sorts of cosmetics, on sexy lingerie, and designer tops.

This type of life was more real to me than my former life in the course of which I had never stepped into a nightclub. I had started very early in my life to be with men. Seeing in me a tasty prey, they sniffed and signalled. Indicating to them my willingness, I would then follow them.

For example, I learned that we could find older and wealthier men in Österhof. Or a bar called Rich was full of divorced Swedish men who, like hunters, were after new prey. Their heads kept turning round and round like hydraulic wheels, and their eyes shone like pairs of searchlights to find what they were after. Spotting us, they would then track us the way the male animals on heat do.

Whenever their faces were too close to my face, their mouths smelt of cheap alcohol mixed with stomach gas and snus that gave me nausea like a poison that would spread all over my body. Many were lonely and losers, one way or another, with their lives on the rocks. They were all lonely after giving all they had to their wives – their villas, Volvo cars, everything – and now they were worse than us. I soon discovered that Swedish men talked about sex all the time, reminding one of the male peacocks that display their plumage to attract females. However, I could easily detect the stupidity and weaknesses in their voices or how depressed they were. Often they drank so much alcohol that they forgot where they were. Having become impotent, many of them fired blanks. They were unable to hit the target, making me laugh at their feeble manhood. Like a heartless whore I laughed at them with contempt. Often they said it was due to their drunkenness that they were unable to have sex. Unable to do anything during the action and look crippled, they resorted to using their mouths or hands to finish the job. That was the most revolting part of the whole game, after which you could shut your eyes and, after an orgasm, press your legs together and kick them off yourself. How enjoyable was the revenge when your wounds were still throbbing! I now understand why no one wants to show her natural face during sexual intercourse.

I saw Johan from time to time, only in my dreams. As time passed, I realized that he was the worst of them all because he had given me hope. There was such a rage inside me that it could destroy everything. I gratified it with my sadomasochistic sex with men. After every orgasm, I wanted to shove my finger into my throat, make myself sick and vomit over them. I held Johan responsible for every misfortune that came my way. He was the cause of my wretchedness. After him, I slept with countless numbers of men. My first encounter with them was the last one; that was all I wanted.

'The way you're acting is quite normal,' Goli told me one day. 'Not to worry. Being in a hurry, people these days are after quick sex. They don't even have time to go to bed or have a meaningful relationship. So don't get emotionally tangled. You won't be hurt if you don't fall in love.'

How could I fall in love with a heart as cold as ice? Having been embittered by hatred, I had become downhearted. I could see that hatred had done something to my body. Having become super active, my mind kept telling me I was a hateful creature. Like one of those cartoon characters, I had become devoid of human emotions – an empty shell with no feelings. Often I wanted to cry, but my eyes were dry. Sleeping with strangers I had just met, I only borrowed their bodies. I took immense pleasure in doing things that others would not normally do. It was as though I enjoyed inflicting pain on myself. I enjoyed anal sex, which made things easier. Women have a vagina, men have a penis, and we are all designed to fulfil the sexual act.

Being driven by possible madness, I kept betraying not him but myself. I knew I wasn't a slut. No, I wasn't a slut. A slut is someone who is with both lovers at the same time. The target of my betrayal was no one but myself.

To put it in another way, I was committing sexual suicide. But, of course, human beings don't only kill themselves by putting a bullet in their heads or swallowing a handful of tablets. There are one thousand ways and means to commit suicide – a gradual one, a social one, and a sexual one. According to Émile Durkheim, there are four types of suicide – fatalistic, anomic, egoistic, and altruistic.

There was a time that I liked someone to look after me, someone strong who could lift me. What I wanted now was someone who would kick me to the bottom of the abyss. I was now sure I no longer belonged to this world. This revelation was beyond my belief. Having lost everything, I had become living proof of a desperate woman in the real world. I had now lost everything in this world, including Danial.

The days had grown longer, and the nights had grown shorter. Winter had gone, and a sudden heat wave from southern Europe forced people to wear thin bright clothes to welcome the unexpected, early summer. The clocks had been moved one hour back, and it didn't get very dark.

'We no more have darkness so that we can slide our small fingers on the taught skin of night,' Goli said one day with a sigh.

'You still remember the poems of Forough Farrokhzaad?' I said.

'Well, of course,' she replied. 'I'll never forget them. How about you?' I recited the whole poem for her:

> *I'm filled with sorrow.*
> *I step onto the terrace*
> *And slide my fingers*
> *On the taught skin of the night.*
> *The lights of my relationship are out.*
> *No one will introduce me to sunshine.*
> *No one will invite me to the sparrows' banquet.*
> *Remember the flight,*
> *The bird will die one day.*

On entering a nightclub one night, we went straight to the bar without queuing to hand over our overcoats and coats to the cloakroom. Wearing a short, white décolleté dress and high-heeled shoes, I followed Goli to the bar. As usual, nearly the same boring men were all there. By now, I had recognised many of them by name or appearance.

'Are you going to promise me to keep calm?' Goli asked me all of a sudden.

'I know; Johan is here, isn't he?'

'That's right,' she answered. 'Look who he's sitting with.'

My heart started beating as hard as I had been running a long distance. '

'Turn around calmly and look at the sonofabitch,' she said.

I saw him sitting near the glass-door. At first, I couldn't believe it was him. Then, I looked more carefully at the area near the exit door. It was Johan sitting on one of the high stools, talking to a blond woman. She had crossed her long legs in a coy manner. Soon I gathered from how she whispered and how they looked at one another passionately that it was not the first time they had met. I was pretty sure that he hadn't seen me.

'Are you all right?' Goli asked.

'What's the time?' I asked.

'Why do you want to know the time?' she said, surprised. 'We've just come.'

'Don't say anything,' I said. 'Just tell me the time!'

The woman lifted her right leg and put it on her left one. Johan shifted a bit on his stool to give some space for her legs. As he turned his face a little, he saw me for an instant and eyed me all over, raising his fair eyebrows. He showed no reaction, as if he had made a mistake. Looking like two glass marbles, his eyes appeared to have opened wide in the dim light. I stared into his eyes and saw in them no emotion, no yearning desire, and no sign of a guilty conscience. It was as though the pupils of his eyes were replaced with two crystals. While I was in torment, he kept calm and quickly turned his face away.

'I want to go home,' I told Goli.

'Now?'

'Yes, right now!'

'Don't show any weakness like a wretch!' she advised. 'How can we go if we've just come? No, we stay put!'

'I'm off,' I said.

At first, I thought Goli would disagree, but after seeing how determined I was, she gave in. Without saying a word, she followed me, finding her way through the crowd.

The music was now blaring, and the disco was on. To get to the entrance door, I had to pass by him. Once more, I looked at his eyes, which had gone yellowish, turning red like traffic lights as the disco lights changed colour. When I passed him, he pretended he didn't know me. Seeing him again was like stopping at the red traffic lights in my life.

Once outside, I took a deep breath. The shops were open, and people were wandering, looking in the shop windows or shopping. A little girl with brown, umbrella-like hair and bright eyes was pushing her pram with her doll in it. Her mother was walking a few steps behind her. The little girl stopped, made her doll comfortable in the pram and started walking again. I said to myself to come to a halt does not mean an end and not every voyage should end up in a destination. I must stop the pain at some point. I must not go on living with this torment. By the same token I must part with some people and finish with them for ever. This failure, for which I had paid a high price, was an experience from which I had learned a lot. Enough was enough now. It was now time I returned to my true self. I had to do that.

I burst into loud laughter.

'Are you crying?' Goli asked.

'I will go back,' I laughed even louder.

'What for?' she asked. 'To slap him? Smashing! Go back there and box his ears. Hit him so hard that he gets humiliated in front of that woman.'

'No, I'll return,' I repeated.

I said to myself I must return right now. But, of course, this momentary stalling didn't mean the end. Still, it signified a new understanding to launch into a new voyage. This time in the form of a transformed human being with a more profound knowledge of my existence on this planet. I knew my exile hadn't started by putting on my clothes and setting off on a journey. The earth had always seemed like an ever-growing tangled skein—no need to set off to another place or country. I want to stay put wherever I am, that's all. It doesn't make any difference where you end up on this earth!

'I knew you would go back to Iran,' Goli exclaimed. 'You want to leave me alone in this hellhole?'

'No.'

'I get it. You want to go to America?'

'No, I'll not go anywhere.'

'I want to go back where I started from.'

'Have you gone nuts?' she said, shaking.

'On the contrary,' I said. 'Just listen to what I have to say.' I put my feet together, stretched my arms out, turned round on the cobblestones and continued: 'I like this air, and I like Stockholm. So I've given up on going to America. I've said goodbye to the idea of returning to my country. I've abandoned the thought of ever being with him.'

'Are you going to say goodbye to me too?' Goli asked.

'My good Iranian friend,' I said, hugging her tightly. 'I've set myself free. I only want one thing. Do you know what it is?' And that was my son.

12

In one of his letters to his fiancée, Felicia, Kafka wrote: 'Have you ever experienced the joy of solitude – to walk alone in the sunshine and lie down in a quiet spot? What bliss for an injured soul, the heart, and the mind! Do you understand what I'm saying? To be able to enjoy a solitary life means that you've had both afflictions and joys in your former life. When I was a little boy, I lived a lonely life determined by my circumstances, not by my choice. But now I dash towards solitude like a river flows down to the sea.'

I hear the chirping of a cricket that falls silent after a moment. The sun is hiding behind the clouds. I get up and see that most people have already gone. Sitting in the shade of a tree where the man-with-a-pram sat before, who had also gone, Danial was eating the food in the bag. I picked up my things and walked up to him.

As Danial was feeling a bit cold, I wrapped him in a towel and looked at him. Spending my days and nights with him, I enjoy his presence beside me. I must confess I've reached the kind of nirvana that Buddha had talked about, just like Siddhartha, who believed that tranquillity and freedom depend on controlling the mind and not on other external conditions. That perfect state of mind can only be found in the 'here and now and not in a faraway realm or a situation beyond the moment we live. I have now accepted to go on with the rest of my life in this state of mind. A life free from unexpected events steeped in an unquestioning acceptance of daily humdrum life devoid of the spice of being adventurous. Having paid a high price for restoring my authentic self and getting Danial back, I guess that's sufficient!

Bless the memory of my grandmother, who said, 'We either shed our skin like a snake or tear our cocoon like a caterpillar.' She always spoke wisely, and now I understand the meaning of her words; that every change is accompanied by pain.

I am happy now. I work hard and earn reasonably good wages. I fulfil my motherhood duties and surpass what is expected from a mother.

I take out the scraps of food from the bag and hand over to Danial what remains from the sandwich and say to him: 'Run along and throw this to the birds. After that, we had to go back home. Granny is waiting for us.

Auntie Goli and Lilian are coming to our home, and she will leave Lilian to stay with us tonight.'

After my father passed away, my mother sold the house and moved to a smaller flat. She spends half of each year with Danial and me. My uncle has also sold Isaac's home in California. With the money I received from the sale of both houses, I could buy a house with a large yard in the Dendrid area near auntie Goli's. She still believes she will never find a man who she can trust. She now has a sweet little daughter who I look after some weekends while Goli goes off to 'have a good time' as she puts it. I still haven't plucked up the courage to tell her that it has been a while since Johan has begun sending me texts!

The protagonist of my tale has gone long ago, and I have replaced her. But, unfortunately, you cannot stop some people from going out of your life. The question is not just about their disappearance; their memories also fade as time passes. The saddest thing is that even those grey spots that are reminders of the inception or incident of love vanish sooner or later.

I haven't seen Johan for more than three years now. I had only seen his full-length photo a few times, showing him wearing a suit with the same cuffs and clasping his hands alongside the articles he had published in the Dagens Bladet and Metro papers. Without reading or keeping those papers, I had crumpled and chucked them in the bin. Last year before Christmas, I received a message wishing Danial and me a Happy New Year, but I didn't reply. But he sent a few more messages which I still didn't answer. So I don't know. The problem is that I had no idea when he would come back, when he would go when he wanted to start again, and when he tried to end again. I'm terrified he might drag me down once again to the hideous abyss of his being and not being with me. Anyway, knowing precisely what I want, I have made up my mind. It has been a long time since I have been in a relationship or had sex with anyone. Having lost count of the length of time I've lived like this, I don't think I will ever be ready to start having sex with anyone again.

Holding a piece of wood between its teeth, a dog runs ahead of its owner, a middle-aged man. The dog comes close to Danial and circles around him.

'Hello,' the man says after a pause.

I answer his greeting. Scared a little, Danial steps backwards. I walk up to him and stand before him.

'Don't be scared,' the man says. 'It's harmless!'

The dog is now robbing itself against Danial's legs, and he is gently stroking the dog's back.

'It's probably going to rain,' the man says, looking at me.

'That's right,' I smile. 'Just like the people here, the weather is unpredictable.'

'Unpredictable!'

'Yes!'

'Exactly,' the man says with a smile. He then points at a villa beside the lake and adds: 'I live there. Do you also live near here?'

I throw the food bag over my shoulder, grab Danial's chubby fingers and walk towards my car, which is parked in the car park.

'Goodbye,' I say to the man before I set off.

Glossary

Allah-o akbar: God is great

Basiji: a member of the paramilitary volunteer militia, Basij, established after the Islamic Revolution. The Basij receive their orders from and subordinate to the Revolutionary Guards.

Chador: means 'tent'. An open black cloak or veil covers the head and the entire body.

En: an article in Swedish that means 'one.'

Ett: an article in Swedish that means 'one.'

Hawz: an ornamental pond in the middle of a courtyard of traditional Persian houses used for washing, floating fruits, and ablutions.

Khodaa haafez: means: God protect/be with you. Goodbye

Khoobi: Are you all right? How are you getting on?

Hejdå: bye-bye in Swedish

Salaam: hello

viyaraaneh: a dish especially prepared to satisfy the cravings of a pregnant woman

Yaa-Allah: means 'O God! O, Allah!' It is said when one politely asks permission to enter a house or a room. It is also displayed when you urge someone to do something.

Asemana Books is devoted to publishing diasporic,
underrepresented, and progressive literature on the Middle East.

asemanabooks.ca

ASEMANA
BOOKS